Miracles Are
Made of This

First published by O Books, 2009
O Books is an imprint of John Hunt Publishing Ltd., The Bothy, Deershot Lodge, Park Lane, Ropley,
Hants, SO24 0BE, UK
office1@o-books.net
www.o-books.net

Distribution in:

UK and Europe
Orca Book Services
orders@orcabookservices.co.uk
Tel: 01202 665432 Fax: 01202 666219
Int. code (44)

USA and Canada
NBN
custserv@nbnbooks.com
Tel: 1 800 462 6420 Fax: 1 800 338 4550

Australia and New Zealand
Brumby Books
sales@brumbybooks.com.au
Tel: 61 3 9761 5535 Fax: 61 3 9761 7095

Far East (offices in Singapore, Thailand,
Hong Kong, Taiwan)
Pansing Distribution Pte Ltd
kemal@pansing.com
Tel: 65 6319 9939 Fax: 65 6462 5761

South Africa
Alternative Books
altbook@peterhyde.co.za
Tel: 021 555 4027 Fax: 021 447 1430

Text copyright Julia Heywood 2008

Design: Stuart Davies

ISBN: 978 1 84694 215 0

A CIP catalogue record for this book is available
from the British Library.

Printed by Digital Book Print

O Books operates a distinctive and ethical publishing philosophy in
all areas of its business, from its global network of authors to
production and worldwide distribution.
This book is produced on FSC certified stock, within ISO14001
standards. The printer plants sufficient trees each year through
the Woodland Trust to absorb the level of emitted carbon in
its production.

Miracles Are Made of This

Julia Heywood

Author of The Barefoot Indian

BOOKS

Winchester, UK
Washington, USA

CONTENTS

Chapter 1

HOME AND AWAY

Well, I finally did it! I successfully achieved the ultimate. After an extensive training program, I passed with flying colors and qualified as Messiahress. But I must add here that part of achieving this ultimate promotion was to arrive at the realization that there is no such thing as a Messiah/Messhiaress. This title is just a label given to those who have discovered Self and demonstrated their 'Unlimited' abilities, it is a label given, usually by those who have not yet fully understood just how extraordinary they themselves are. When it is fully grasped that there is no thing greater than and no thing less than self, then Saviours are a thing of the past.

As part of my training, I was assigned a beautiful guide and mentor, The Barefoot Indian, who assisted me on my journey, and I am forever grateful to her. I was also in direct contact with Head Office and its wonderful beings who tirelessly work from there. They too were a constant source of inspiration as I ventured along my path.

Head Office is the center of excellence. It is located on the top floor of the tallest of buildings and is designed to give a bird's eye view of the world. From there all things can be seen, from there everything makes sense. Its location is at the heart of everything. There you will find all the great prophets, philosophers, gurus, sages, enlightened beings, spiritual teachers – whatever you want to label them – all those who have painstakingly walked the earth and lovingly shared their knowledge with those of us who are willing to hear.

So, it is from Head Office that the next chapter of my story begins. Head Office was my home now and it was where I belonged…

It was still like a dream to me that I should find myself at Head Office, little old me, ordinary, simple and at times a bit dim, but not any more (well that's not strictly true!). I had seen the light; I had seen what all these wonderful people who reside here had also seen, and if I could see it then anybody could see it.

It was so amazing to hang around with these people, I felt like I could spend every day listening to them talk and hearing their stories. Their sense of humor was such that I laughed so hard my jaw and stomach ached and tears rolled down my face.

Amongst many stories, they shared their tales of what lengths they had gone to in pursuit of enlightenment and almost treated it as a competition, with me as judge, to see who had engaged in the most ridiculous things, all of which had resulted in no enlightenment whatsoever. Although, I would have to say that in a way, it did result in enlightenment, for to realize that their pursuits were not getting them anywhere and consequently to give up on those ideas, was in itself enlightenment.

One story in particular comes to mind. I will not say who it was to save embarrassment, but this happened many, many years ago. This is what he said.

"I decided that it would be a good idea to sit and meditate upon a brick wall. I reasoned that I needed something to focus on, to empty my head of all thoughts and concentrate on one thing only. If I could understand the essence of the wall, I would understand everything. So, I gave up everything in my life and rid myself of all distractions. Amongst many things, I gave up love, comfort and money and went in pursuit of a wall that would suit my purpose."

"Wouldn't any wall have done?" I asked.

"Oh no," he replied seriously. "It had to be in a quiet place where I would not be disturbed and the wall had to be such a height that I could not see over it."

"Oh," I said, trying not to giggle.

2

"I eventually found the wall and began my meditation. I was determined to contemplate it until I was enlightened and to achieve the ultimate; to be able to walk through it," he explained.

"I looked at that wall from every possible angle; sideways, left and right, straight on and I even, at times, stood on my head to get a different view of it. On occasions I tried to put my hands through it, but I just ended up with bruises on my knuckles. There were times though when I thought I was getting somewhere, the wall would appear to shimmer and spin, but I soon realized that that was down to sunstroke!"

"Anyway, to cut a very long story short, eventually, after four very painful years of sitting and staring at the brick wall and feeling very isolated, I suddenly had clarity, I had the break-through. The realization of what I was looking at began to dawn on me. I finally knew what I was staring at."

"And what was it you were staring at?" I asked intrigued.

"A brick wall!" he replied.

To date I have judged this story to be in first place, though this could easily drop in the rankings as more tales come through. I would like to add that after the incident with the brick wall he soon achieved enlightenment, not because of it, but despite it.

The biggest pleasure of being at Head Office was the opportunity to learn from these awesome people. I had already come such a long way, yet there was still an eternity of learning and I could not think of a better way to spend my days.

When I speak of learning it is not to be confused with being at school or of something tortuous, it is more of a constant unfolding of self. Like a flower coming into bloom with each petal that unfolds, there is more to discover.

I was enjoying myself so much at Head Office that I rather hoped that my next challenge could be done from there, and that was my original intention, but I soon found out that there were very few opportunities for me to progress. Having previously passed the exam for Messiahress at level 1 I knew that my next challenge was to pass level 2. This involved practicing and demonstrating everything that I had learnt so far in level 1, and the world did seem to be the perfect classroom to achieve this. However, I really did not want to go out there.

I knew I would not be able to resist the inevitable for much longer when JC the Managing Director approached me one day.

"Have you decided yet to begin your next phase, Level 2?" he asked me.

"Erm...sort of," I replied. "I was wondering, could I not stay here to do it?"

"You could do it anywhere, the choice is yours, but it would take you such a long time to succeed. Planet earth is perfect for your next phase as it is equipped with the tools that you need. It would be far more beneficial for you to go down there and shine," he said, looking out of the window down upon the world.

"What tools do I need?" I enquired.

"Contrast," he answered. "What better place is there to demonstrate love and compassion in a place that appears to be void of such things? For you to discover and understand more of yourself, to shine like a beacon, to know what it means to be light, there is no better place to be than in a place that appears to be in darkness."

I thought about what he was saying and my mind wandered back to the time when The Barefoot Indian came to me as my training coach to guide me. It was true, her wisdom, love and compassion shone like the sun at the side of my ignorance. I was like a blank cinema screen which allowed her to project all that she knew on to it giving us both the opportunity to see and learn. The teacher was the pupil and the pupil was the teacher.

I brought myself back to the present and turned to JC. "I guess you're right." I said.

"I guess so," he said smiling.

I moved next to him at the window and stared down upon the world. People were going about their business, oblivious that

Head Office even existed. If only they knew what was here, their fear would dissolve, they would be free, they would live as they have never lived before, I thought to myself.

"Why doesn't anybody acknowledge Head Office?" I asked JC. "I mean it's so huge that you can hardly miss it can you? People must be blind!"

"You missed it for quite some time," he replied. "Why was that?"

"Point taken," I said sheepishly.

I thought about this for a short while and then concluded, "I guess I was so preoccupied with my own little selfish world, it never occurred to me that there was a greater meaning, a greater understanding. It was only when I could no longer continue living the way I was, that Head Office became apparent to me."

"Was it ever thus!" said JC.

"I have noticed though that young children occasionally look up and wave at us," I continued. "Why is that?"

"They still remember us. Although a very faint memory, they can still remember where they came from," he replied. "But that memory will fade even further as they become more, as you say, preoccupied."

"We are sending out signs all the time for people to acknowledge us, yet no one seems to be reading them at the moment. It is very quiet. It would be good for you to go out there and try to wake a few people up."

"But," I said, "and this is a big BUT, when I have looked at the lives of those who have been in the world and tried to, as you say, 'wake a few people up', terrible things seem to happen to them. Two events come straight to mind; death by Hemlock, nails and crosses! I do not fancy any of that!"

"Ah yes," he said laughing. "It can appear to be terrible, but as you know by now, you cannot believe everything you hear or read. Having been there myself, let me show you what happened to me from my perspective."

5

With that he placed his hand on my forehead and instantly my mind was transported back in time. I was looking at the whole of his life being played out like a film. I watched with interest as the film progressed and his life flashed in front of me as if in a moment. When it was over, he removed his hand from my forehead and looked at me as I stood in awe.

"Well?" he asked.

"Wow, that's so cool!" I said. "So that's how it was for you. That's amazing!"

"As you've just seen, everything happened exactly as I wanted it to happen and only I know what that was," he said.

"My message was a simple one."

"Yes, I can see that," I said. "But wouldn't it be useful for everyone to know how it was for you?"

"It doesn't matter," he replied. "It's my life, from my perspective. The whole point of existence is to know oneself. What would it profit someone to know everything about me, yet know nothing of themselves? But should anyone be so curious as to want to know about me and my experiences then they will have to come to me and ask me, just as you have done."

"Yes, I understand," I said smiling.

After seeing his life from his perspective, I started to feel a little less anxious about my impending fate.

After a few moments JC asked, "So are you now ready to go out there and glow?"

"I suppose so," I said reluctantly.

"Go on then," he said.

"What, NOW?" I said, alarmed.

"Yes," he nodded. "There's no time like the present."

"But...I'm not ready yet," I exclaimed.

"Why not?" he asked.

"Because...because..." I muttered, but I couldn't really think of a reason.

"Go on then," he said. "Have fun! Remember we will be

6

observing your progress along the way."

"How long will I be out there?" I asked. "How long will it take for me to pass Level 2?"

"However long it takes!" he said in a knowing tone. "We will come for you when the task is completed."

"That's very kind of you," I said sarcastically.

With that he put his arm around me and started to direct me to the door. I reluctantly walked with him, knowing I really did not have a choice.

"As you know, there is nothing that you cannot do. You know who and what you are: 'The Unlimited'," he said softly. "We are with you every step of the way."

"I understand," I said, "But I wish I could stay."

"You'll love it out there," he said. "I promise. You have seen how it was for me and the enlightening times I had!"

He reached inside his pocket and pulled out a cell phone which he handed to me.

"Take this with you," he said. "You'll need it."

"Whatever for?" I asked in surprise.

"We will text you," he replied. "On occasions we may send you advice should you need it, and maybe a few jokes just because we can!"

"Ok," I said, putting the cell phone into my handbag.

Others had gathered by the door to bid their farewells. The door opened and I hesitantly began to walk through it backwards.

"Bye then," I said blowing them kisses. "I hope to see you all very soon."

"Goodbye," they all shouted in unison.

As I turned to walk out of the door I was certain I felt JC's foot kicking me on my butt, pushing me on my way. I spun around to look at him and he was standing there all innocent with a broad grin on his face. He winked at me just before the Head Office door closed firmly.

So that was it, I was on my way, level 2 had commenced. As I made my way out of the building I was already thinking about the day when I would return.

Chapter 2

THE GRASS IS ALWAYS GREENER...

I left Head Office and crossed over the road to walk through the park. I had no thought of where I was going or what I was going to do. The weather was warm and sunny and there was not a cloud in the sky. The park was scattered with people taking in the sun's rays, everybody seemed cheerful and relaxed. I glanced around and found myself looking back up towards the top of the tower at the 'Unlimited Suite'. I could see all my friends looking down on me, smiling and waving. 'There is no point in looking back,' I thought to myself. 'The quicker I complete level 2, the quicker I can return.' With that I found a spring in my step and carried on walking ahead.

Whilst walking I just contemplated putting one foot in front of the other, which is always a nice little exercise to do when you want to be focused. Apart from the birds singing loudly, every-thing was so peaceful. By now I was relaxing into the inevitable. 'This challenge is going to be so easy,' I reassured myself. 'If every day is like this then I have nothing to worry about.'

I slowly meandered through the park, taking in my surroundings. I was feeling very chilled out and at one with everything so I decided to sit for a while on the grass and observe the world going by. I had just made myself comfortable when I heard laughing and giggling. I glanced around and noticed a group of children playing together a short distance away. Their innocence caught my attention and I watched them with interest.

My thoughts were soon interrupted by a grumpy voice

"Bloody annoying, aren't they," said a man who had decided to plonk himself down next to me. "All that noise really gets on my nerves, especially as I have a headache."

I must add here that I seem to be one of those people who can enter an empty train carriage and I could guarantee that the next person to board would sit next to me. Why that is, I have no idea. They could sit anywhere, but I must have that sort of face that says 'Please come and talk to me'. Anyway, I digress.

I turned to the man. "Why don't you move and go somewhere else?" I asked him. "This park is so vast, I'm sure you can find a quiet spot."

"Why should I move? I have a right to be here," he said grumpily. "In fact I have more of a right to be here than them."

"Oh really," I said in surprise. "Why do you say that?"

"Well I'm older and wiser," he answered abruptly.

"Oh really," I said again, a little taken aback by his arrogance. "I would have to disagree with that. From where I'm sitting, they are far wiser than you."

"Impossible!" he declared. "I've lived a full life and I've gained a lot of knowledge along the way. I could teach them a thing or two," he said smugly.

"If you say so," I said. "However, I think they could teach you more."

"What do you mean?" he asked half-heartedly.

"Well, for example, when was the last time you were carefree like them?"

The man looked at me strangely, but couldn't answer, so I continued talking; I was on a roll.

"When was the last time you laughed like them? When was the last time you played like them? When was the last time you experienced joy like them? When was the last time you were free from worry? When was the last time each day was a new adventure to you? When was the last time you were trusting? When was the last time your life was as uncomplicated as theirs?"

On and on I went, the words just kept tumbling from my mouth. I couldn't help it, I was desperate for him to see how he had shrouded the child within him with fears and preconceived ideas.

It didn't need to be this way. Eventually, I could tell by the man's face that he was beginning to see the fundamental error in his thinking. I decided to shut up, but not before concluding, "So you see, I think they have more to teach you if you are willing to learn from them. Be like a child. Strive to be as them: simple, innocent and pure in thought."

After a few moments of silence he turned to me and said in a sad tone, "I can't remember the last time my life was like theirs."

"So of what use to you is all the supposed knowledge you say you've gained along the way?" I asked.

He thought for some time and then replied, "I guess it's of no use. All it has seemed to have done is stop me from having fun. It has stopped me from being carefree; stopped me from living. In fact, to be honest, it has made me bloody miserable!"

I said no more and allowed the man time to contemplate our conversation. He was deep in thought as he watched the children playing. His face was becoming more relaxed as he continued to observe them and he was definitely looking less grumpy.

Suddenly he turned to me and exclaimed. "My headache has gone!"

"Your headache was nothing more than placing your head in an imaginary vice with your own hands tightening it," I told him.

The man nodded in agreement. We sat in silence and continued to watch the children play. I was marvelling at their god-like qualities when, as if by some divine intervention, just to prove me wrong, all hell broke loose. They started shouting and screaming at one another and arguing amongst themselves, some of them began to cry. They had obviously fallen out over something trivial so I decided to intervene.

"What's going on?" I asked as I approached them

I was hit with a tirade of 'he said this...' 'she did that...' 'that's not fair...' After quietening them down and getting to the bottom of what was going on, it became apparent that they were arguing over who should be on whose team. According to them, some were better than others. They were discriminating.

"Will you do something for me?" I asked them all.

"Yes," they replied reluctantly, but at last they had stopped arguing.

"Go over there," I said pointing to an area of grass, "and find me two blades of grass that are the same as each other, then bring them to me."

"Ok!" The children were suddenly excited as they ran off to begin the task.

"They must be the same in every way, though," I shouted out to them.

To my surprise the 'grumpy' man asked if he could join in, and he did. I was thrilled that he wanted to play.

I left them all to it, sat back down and watched them as they rummaged around the grass in search of identical blades. They were engrossed in the activity and oblivious to one another. This must have gone on for a few hours and as time was pressing on I decided to interrupt them.

"Have you found what you were looking for?" I asked as I approached.

"No," they said in unison.

"We cannot find two blades of grass that are the same," said one of them, "they are all different."

"Yet, are they not all blades of grass?" I asked.

Without waiting for an answer I continued talking. "Does the sun only shine on the best blade of grass? The one it prefers? The one that is the strongest?"

"No," they said in a 'that's obvious' tone. "It shines on all of them."

"And does the rain only pour on the most deserving blade of grass? The one that drinks the most? The one that is the greenest?" I asked.

"No, it rains on all of them," they said.

12

"So, no matter how different each blade of grass is, the sun and rain sees them as the same and treats them equally?" I asked.

"Yes," they agreed.

"And why does the sun shine on all of them? And why does the rain pour on all of them?" I enquired.

They were silent for a few minutes and you could see their little minds searching for the answer. Finally one of them said, "I don't know. It just seems to happen that way."

"That's right, it just happens that way. That's the way it is." I said. "And so it is with you. You are like the blades of grass, it doesn't matter how different you are, you are the same. There is no blade of grass which is greater than another, each blade is unique. You are all viewed in exactly the same way. That's the way it is. All life is equal and should be treated as such. Just as the sun and rain nurtures the grass as one, so too does life bless you. Do you understand?"

"Yes, we do," they said giggling.

"Now go play and put into practice what you know," I said, and they did in perfect harmony.

The 'grumpy' man came over to me

"That was an interesting exercise," he said. "I really understood something."

"And what did you understand?" I asked, eyebrows arched.

"It seems that no matter how different we appear to be, in essence, we are all the same and problems only arise when we don't acknowledge that."

"Well done," I said smiling.

Again, he fell silent for some time in contemplation, then suddenly he said, "I've had the most fascinating day. I feel like a child again!"

"Great!" I said. "Keep working on it."

"I will," he said. "I promise."

The children continued to play as I made my move to leave. "I am going now," I said to the 'grumpy' man.

"Oh what a shame," he said. "I've really enjoyed myself today."

"So have I!" I said smiling as I turned to walk away. "Good bye," I said, but as I was leaving him I was stopped in my tracks and was compelled to turn around and say, "We shall meet again. You will know the place and time."

"OK," he said looking a little bemused. "Bye for now."

However, he was not as bemused as I was. Why did I say that? I thought to myself as I walked away.

I made my way to the park gates. I was feeling slightly proud of myself and was rather looking forward to the next challenge. I always believe in easing myself in gently and that was a perfect start to level 2. It was just enough to make a difference.

As I was leaving the park I suddenly heard the sound of heavenly bells ringing; they were playing *Hallelujah.* I looked around to see where they were coming from, but was unable to find the source. They were getting louder and louder with each moment, then it dawned on me that it was my cell phone ringing. 'Someone has got a terrible sense of humor,' I thought to myself, 'I must change that hideous ring-tone!' I reached inside my handbag and pulled out the cell phone. It was a text message. I found a nearby wall and sat down as I eagerly read the message.

Message from Head Office:

Well done! As we have always said, wise people talk because they have something to say and fools talk because they have to say something.
Also, you can discover more about a person in an hour of play than in a year of conversation.
Wheresoever you go, go with all your heart.
Speak 2U soon x x x

Having read the text, I placed the phone back in to my handbag and in doing so I became aware that my old notebook was inside, the one I had used throughout my earlier training. I pulled it out to take a look. I flicked through the pages and smiled as I reminisced over my notes and realized how helpful they were all through the training in level 1. In realizing this the thought occurred to me that I should make notes as I progress through level 2. So with eagerness I fumbled through my handbag in search of a pen, and on finding it I continued to sit for a while and contemplated the events of the day. I then headed the page and began to write.

What I demonstrated today...

Find the child within

All things are equal

Chapter 3

CLIFF HANGER

I had been on level 2 for about two weeks and to be honest, very little was happening. I had engaged in the occasional conversation, but apart from that, zilch, nothing. I therefore decided to practice on my own. I needed to brush up, to become more advanced on moving without limitation, so that is what I did.

I visited some amazing places from deserts to mountain tops without all the hassle of catching flights or walking boots. There are so many wonderful sights to see on earth, but many go unnoticed due to the insistence of time and space. Anyway, it didn't take me too long to master the art, I was finding it very easy to move the body from one place to another as quick as the blinking of an eye, however, I felt as though I needed a greater challenge; to do something that was new to me.

'I know!' I thought to myself suddenly, 'I shall practice being the wind, I have not done that before and I think it could be fun.' Now, I know this may sound far fetched, but trust me, everything is experiential!

I sat quietly and allowed the experience of the wind to arise within me. It took sometime before the feeling came, but once it did, wow, I was off like a torpedo.

The feeling was indescribable, though I shall try to explain it. I was like thin air yet solid at the same time and I was without a beginning or an end; I was boundless. I could move as fast or as slowly as I desired. When I came across a tree it felt as though the tree passed straight through me and as it did I shook all the dead debris from within the tree, like giving it a spring clean. Dead branches and leaves were tossed to the ground with ease. Nothing could stop me and nothing could challenge me. As I made my way across the land gathering speed and energy, I could clearly see that no matter how big the ego of man was, humans were unable to contain me, to own me, to decide my fate. Humans could try for a million years, yet could never succeed. It was awesome.

I was having so much fun being the wind, experiencing the experience, that I was becoming more and more oblivious to the world around me, yet as I was moving along a particular stretch of coast, something suddenly caught my attention. I slowed down and observed a man who was standing right on the edge of a very high cliff. He appeared to be very angry and upset and was screaming out, but nobody was there. My curiosity got the better of me and I decided to investigate further. I slowed right down to a gentle breeze and got as close as I could without knocking him off the edge.

"God," he screamed at the sky. "Why have you done this to me. What have I done to deserve this?"

He paused for a moment to catch his breath and to wipe his tears. "If you don't answer me, I shall jump."

'Oh dear,' I thought, 'I think I'd better help him.'

I brought myself back to my usual self and stood behind him, but not too close as I did not want to startle him, he was very close to the edge – in more ways than one.

I gently called out his name and he spun around.

"Who are you?" he asked in surprise. "How do you know my name?"

I didn't answer him, instead I moved slowly towards him and held out my hand for him to take.

"Go away," he said. "I want to be alone."

I withdrew from him and said, "Very well, but is it Ok if I stand here and watch?"

He looked at me in a puzzled way, shrugged his shoulders and then turned his head to look back at the sky. He then continued with his rant.

"God...."

I interrupted him. "Why are you talking to the sky?" I asked.

Again, he spun around to look at me. "Are you still here?" he said. "What do you want? Why do you want to watch? Are you some kind of sicko?"

"I'm just curious, that's all, I want to see whether you jump or not," I replied, and then added, "although it doesn't matter to me if you do or don't."

He turned away, ignoring me and continued to shout at the sky.

"God..."

Again I interrupted him. "You didn't answer me. Why are you talking to the sky?"

He spun his head around. "I am not talking to the sky," he said sarcastically. "I am talking to God."

"But God is not in the sky," I said.

"OK clever clogs," he said smugly whilst turning to face me. "Tell me where he is then."

"I am looking at him." I said staring directly at his eyes.

The man fell silent and looked into my eyes for the first time, but then quickly looked away.

"If you are going to enter into a dialogue with God," I continued, "then it would make sense to find out where he is first, don't you agree?"

The man didn't reply, but just looked down at his feet. After a short while he decided to speak to me.

"What do you know? You know nothing about me and my situation."

"I am not really interested in your situation, although you are and I think that is your problem."

"What do you mean when you say 'that's my problem?'" he asked.

"What I mean is you are too interested in your own situation."

"In what way?" he said smugly "Would you care to expand on

that?"

"Ok," I said, "How many people do you think there are in the world who have or are experiencing the same situation as you?"

He thought about this for a while and then said, "I don't know, I guess there could be hundreds, maybe thousands."

"And does it bother you that they are suffering? Do you stand and shout at the sky for each and every one of them?"

"No," he said slightly embarrassed, but then continued, "It doesn't bother me that they suffer. I am only bothered when it is personal to me."

"So the situation itself does not bother you, it is only when you say it is personal to you that the problem arises?" I asked him.

"Erm… well yes, I suppose so," he replied, looking down towards the ground again.

He thought about this and as he did he began to relax. In an interested tone he suddenly asked, "What should I do about it?"

"Stop trying to make things personal."

"How do I do that?" he enquired.

"By realizing that you don't need to. If you could fully understand for one moment your true self, your natural state, making things personal would be a thing of the past," I replied.

"What do mean, my true self? What is my true self?"

"I shall show you." I fumbled in my handbag and pulled out my *Witwai* ball and passed it to him. The *Witwai* ball is the world in miniature, it's the size of a tennis ball and is spongy in texture.

"Take this," I said as I passed the ball to him. "Hold this ball in your hands. This ball replicates the world. Just point out to me on the ball where in the world you say you are. Place yourself on the ball."

He pointed to an area on the ball.

"And how small are you in relation to the ball?" I asked.

"I am microscopic," he replied.

"And all your problems, emotions and the things that are personal to you, how small are they in relation to the ball?"

"Even more microscopic, they appear to be totally insignif-icant!" he declared.

"Good!" I said and then continued, "Now let's turn our attention to the one who is holding the ball. How big are you in relation to the ball?"

"I am huge, I am vast, the ball is very small," he said.

"Can you see the whole of the ball?" I asked.

"Yes, I can see all of it."

"So everything that is happening on the ball is visible to you."

"Yes, but it's so tiny it is hardly visible and seems so unimportant, in fact I'm not so sure anything is going on. If it is then it is of no significance to me," he said.

"So which would you rather be, the miniscule person on the ball who is concerned with personalizing fears and emotions that are even less visible, or the huge, vast entity that is holding the ball?" I asked.

"Well, the one holding the ball, without a doubt," he replied.

"Right answer!" I said. "And this is what your true self is like. You are a vast entity that cannot only see the ball and know everything about it, but you can also see for miles beyond it. You can choose to be aware of the most microscopic or you can choose to be aware of the vastness that's all around. The choice is yours."

He continued to look at the *Witwai* in his hand and was clearly deep in thought.

"Remember what you have just seen. Use the *Witwai* as a meditation tool," I said. "Carry it with you and whenever you feel uncertain, fearful or confused, just hold it in your hands to remind yourself of who you truly are. You need to work on expanding your awareness and altering your perspective. You need to keep reminding yourself of your true identity, your true state, your true potential. These things you have long forgotten. Will you do this?"

"Yes I will," he said excitedly. "Where can I get a *Witwai* from?"

"You can keep that one," I replied, "I have plenty more."

"Thank you," he said, "I think it will be very useful, but can I ask, why is it called a *Witwai*? Is it some sort of ancient, mystical name? Does it have spiritual significance?"

"Not at all!" I said laughing "It simply stands for –**W**here **I**n **T**he **W**orld **A**m **I**."

"Ah, very clever," he said laughing.

He stood for a while looking out to sea and I could tell he was still thinking about the *Witwai*. He then turned to me and said, "I feel much better now. Things are not that bad." He paused to think before continuing. "Actually in truth there is nothing there that can be bad. I feel as though my problems were no bigger than a speck of dust which I have blown away with a puff of breath."

"Brilliant!" I said.

"Can I ask you something else?" he said.

"Sure," I replied.

"Earlier you said it did not matter to you if I jumped or not. Why did you say that? I got the feeling that you meant it."

"I did mean it," I said, "and I shall now show you why."

I walked forward and stepped straight off the cliff edge. I was suspended in what looked to him like mid air. I turned to face him. He stood there with his mouth wide open.

"How…how do you do that?" he stammered.

"How could I not do it?" I asked "There is only God 'the Unlimited', that which I am. When you look over the edge of this cliff, you see the top and the bottom. When I look over the edge of this cliff I see the top, the bottom and the space in between and it's the space in between that holds me up. To me it is solid, to you it's invisible."

"To me it's just air!" he said.

"That may be so, but what is that air?" I said in response. "These are the sort of questions you need to explore. The answers are within you, bring them forth, you do not need to search for them elsewhere and you will know without doubt when you have found them."

He fell silent and then suddenly said, "Yes.. but... if I had jumped I wouldn't have been suspended in mid air. I would have dropped like a brick and crashed to my fate." "That may have been so. But that's Ok, believe it or not, you are eternally safe."

"There's no arguing with you is there?" he said.

"Nope!" I agreed, "One day soon you shall come to know that which supports everything."

He finally walked away from the edge of the cliff and joined me to sit for a while to watch the mist rolling in from the sea. Then he asked, "Where did you come from? You seemed to appear from nowhere."

"The wind brought me here," I said.

"Yeh... right. Seriously, where did you appear from and how did you know my name?" He asked.

"All I have to say is remember the *Witwai*." I said. "When you hold the world in the palm of your hands, anything is possible."

He looked at me and smiled and then looked into his hand at the *Witwai*. I stood up to say goodbye. My task was complete.

"I am going now," I said, "but we shall meet again."

"Will we?" he questioned and before I had time to think the words again just tumbled out of my mouth. "Yes we will. You will know the time and the place."

'Why do I keep saying that?' I wondered to myself. Again I was being compelled to say it, though with no idea why.

"I look forward to it," he said smiling.

"Me too," I said. "See you soon."

"Bye for now," he said as I walked away.

I left him sitting as I made my way along the cliff path. A short while later I turned around and he was walking away in the opposite direction. I decided to sit for a moment to gather my thoughts and reflect on the day's events.

It had been a very eventful day and overall I felt as though I had demonstrated quite a lot of what I knew about myself.

As I was contemplating I was interrupted by the familiar sound of my cell phone ringing, well it wasn't quite ringing, rather it was playing the annoying *Hallelujah* tune which I had not yet managed to work out how to change.

I looked at the screen and saw I had a message. I eagerly opened it and read the following:

Message from Head Office:

What an eventful day you have had!
You have left him wondering and as we say 'wisdom begins in wonder!'
The unexamined life is not worth living.
Congratulations
CU L8R xxx

Whilst the events of the day were still fresh in my mind, I wrote in my notebook:

What I demonstrated today...

Find the child within

All things are equal

Life cannot be contained

Problems are whatever size you want them to be

All life is supported

Chapter 4

A SHINING EXAMPLE!

Having been on my new adventure for some time, I noticed that a pattern was emerging. A day never went by without a place to stay. The generosity of people at times was overwhelming, they welcomed me with open arms, what was theirs was mine and what was mine was theirs. Therefore, it made sense for me to hand my house over to someone else. I needed to do something with it. It had been sitting empty since I qualified and it really needed to be lived in. I no longer required it as I was constantly traveling and was never in one place for very long, so I thought it best that someone else moved in. However, I had to check that everything was in order and to clear out a few bits and pieces.

I decided to walk there as on this particular day I was not too far away and it gave me the opportunity to reminisce about the area that I once lived in. I walked around the lake where The Barefoot Indian first taught me how to walk on water and I couldn't help but smile as I remembered that day. I found a bench and sat for a while and stared into the water. The water was far clearer than I remembered and I could see the fish swimming around at the bottom of the lake. I sat for ages being mesmerised by the movement of the water and, apart from the occasional thoughts of Head Office popping into my mind, everything was perfectly still.

Eventually, I decided it was time to make a move as I wanted to press on with getting the house sorted. I stood up to leave and as I did so, a young woman sitting on a blanket caught my eye. She appeared to be reading a book, but she was merely looking down at it, you could tell she wasn't reading as her mind seemed to be preoccupied. In fact the more I looked at her the more I could see an overwhelming sadness in her face. My heart went out to her and I found myself walking towards her.

"Do you mind if I sit with you for a while?" I asked as I approached her.

She looked up in surprise and stared at me. I could sense that she was about to tell me to go away, but then suddenly she had a change of heart.

"Please yourself," she said in a nonchalant tone.

So I did. I sat next to her, in silence, on the blanket, whilst she continued pretending to read her book. Nothing was said.

Eventually her curiosity got the better of her and she turned to me and asked, "Why did you want to sit with me?"

"Because you looked so sad, I hoped that I could help in some way," I replied.

"Then why didn't you offer me any help when you first approached me?" she asked.

"True help can only be given when you ask for it, not by me offering it," I said.

She thought for a moment

"I am not sure what you mean," she said, questioningly.

"It's like this," I said. "Imagine there is a fountain and the water in the fountain is wisdom, it is the font of all knowledge. On drinking the water, all becomes clear to you, problems dissolve and you are alive once again. If I offer you a drink from the fountain when you are not thirsty, you will turn me down. But if you come to me thirsty, you will take what's on offer and will drink from the fountain." I paused to let that sink in.

"So, my help is available to you, but only if you desire it."

She considered my words and then said with a smile, "I am thirsty!" And after a brief pause she continued, "but I don't know where to begin to explain to you all my problems. Everything I touch seems to end in disaster."

"You don't have to tell me anything," I said. "All is known."

"Is it?" she asked puzzled.

"Yes, take yesterday for example, you lost your job."

"How did you know that?" she said in astonishment. "We've never met before."

"As I said, all is known."

"Wow!" She said. "What else do you know?"

"I know that you have viewed many things in your life as obstacles."

"That's right!" she declared. "My life is full of them."

"That maybe so, but trying to overcome them is where you have been going wrong."

"Isn't that the whole point of an obstacle?" she asked, and then added, "Obstacles have to be overcome."

"Obstacles are not there to be overcome, they are there to tell you to do something else. They are like signposts. It is rather like approaching a river which you would like to cross, but the water is turbulent and too dangerous. It presents you with an obstacle which you say you have to overcome. So you become obsessed with trying to work out how to cross the river by any means possible; altering the course of water to calm it down, building a sturdy raft that will get you across. In the process you wear yourself out. However, if you just stopped for a moment and gave up on your obsession, you would see that all you need to do is move on, find another route, walk further down the river and you will find a calm and shallow spot where you can effortlessly get to the other side to where you want to be."

"So I don't need to overcome them?" she asked.

"No, you just need to do something else. These problems are pointing you in another direction. Move on."

"I've never looked at it in that way before," she said, musing.

"I know!" I smiled. "Now that you are starting to view them that way, your future will unfold very differently from your past."

"Will it?"

"Yes. Your future will be involved with giving. You will be surrounded by young children and you will have plenty to offer them. You will brighten up their days and they will look to you for guidance and security."

"That seems impossible!" she said, "Although I must admit, years ago I did have a desire to work with children, but circumstances didn't allow for it. My life never took me in that direction."

"Perhaps you misread the obstacles," I said, "Start listening to what they are truly saying to you and I can guarantee your life will change."

"Will it?" she asked again.

"Yes."

"I'll give it a go then," she agreed. "I will start to listen to them instead of trying to overcome them."

We both fell silent and she was clearly thinking about her so-called obstacles. I remained silent whilst she was deep in thought.

Suddenly, without any logical reason, she turned to me and asked, "Do you believe in God?"

"Does it matter to you if I do or don't?" I replied. "If I said yes would that help you in any way? And if I said no would that make any difference to you?"

I didn't wait for her to answer, but carried on talking. "I think you are really questioning whether you believe in God or not."

"Yes, I suppose I am," she said thoughtfully. "I don't believe in God, although I think I would like to."

I decided to offer her some clarification. "You don't need to *believe* in God, the 'Unlimited', you simply need to *know* that God, the 'Unlimited' is ever present."

"But how do I do that?" she said, puzzled. "If I could see the 'Unlimited', as you call it, I would know that it was ever present, but I don't see it!"

"You don't need to see it," I said. "Let me put it like this, I shall use the sun as an example. It is a magnificent, awesome ball of pure energy, always radiating warmth and light in a reassuring way. The suns rays radiate all the way across the earth in a single movement, from the one source. Throughout your life it is the one

28

thing that is constant, everyday it is there. It is what it is and it does what it does. Endlessly it gives of itself and asks nothing from you in return, and look at what occurs when you give like that, you illuminate the world."

She nodded in acknowledgment.

I asked her, "Have you ever looked directly at the sun to see if it's there?"

"No."

"Do you need to look at the sun to know it's there?"

"No," she replied.

"Why not?" I asked.

"Because you know it is there, you can feel it. You can feel its rays, its warmth and you experience its light."

"Excellent!" I said, "And that is what the 'Unlimited,' is like. You do not need to see it nor find it in order to know that it is there. You feel it, you experience it, right here, right now. You just *know* it's there, it is as simple as that. Wherever you are, so too will the 'Unlimited' be."

"That's awesome!" she said.

"It is!" I agreed, "Whenever doubt and fear commands your attention, just remember that those emotions are like the clouds which briefly obscure the sun, but the sun is still shining and before long the clouds will evaporate. Move your thoughts to the sun, to that which is ever present. Use the sun as a shining example to God, the 'Unlimited'. It's an excellent tool."

"I will," she said.

"And remember, just like the sun's rays can always be felt, anywhere and everywhere, so too can the love of the 'Unlimited' be experienced."

We sat quietly for a while as she absorbed what had been said. I felt as though I had achieved my objective and prepared myself to leave. I stood up to go as it was time for me to move on, I had quite a lot to do at home.

"Can I ask you one more thing?" she asked suddenly.

"Of course."

"Why do you refer to the 'Unlimited' and not to God?"

"Because to use the word God would limit the 'Unlimited'," I replied smiling. "I shall leave that with you to think about."

"Thanks," she said warmly.

"You're welcome," I said smiling."I am going now, it has been lovely spending time with you."

"I've enjoyed myself too."

"Well, I am sure we will meet again," I said.

"Do you think so?" she said doubtfully.

And before I had time to think, the words just tumbled from my mouth, "Yes, you will know the place and time."

'Why do I keep saying that?' I thought to myself, yet again.

We said our goodbyes and I continued on my journey back to my house.

As I was approaching the front door, my cell phone began to play that ridiculous tune again. Of all the infinite things I was now able to do, I found it impossible to work out how to change that ring tone! I pulled it out from my pocket and read the following message:

Message from Head Office:

We think you are doing really well and would just like to say the following:

Thousands of candles can be lit from a single candle and the life of the candle will not be shortened. Happiness never decreases by being shared.

Neither fire nor wind, birth nor death can erase our good deeds

ATB xxx

What a nice message I thought to myself as I walked through the front door.

I found the house exactly as I had left it, but of course it would be as no one had been living there. The first thing I did was to switch on my beloved computer and I was greeted with the familiar techno voice 'you have mail.'

I eagerly opened the email expecting it to be from Head Office with another message, but it wasn't, it was from my mother (she really is getting the hang of this technology stuff). It was one of her many poems.

To My Dearest Daughter

My earthly life my daughter dear
Was one of great confusion
But now your feet are on 'the path'
I see a wise conclusion
Your words of wisdom
Spoken now in very modern fashion
Still hold the truth of ages past
And fill my heart with passion
I have not found the 'Ultimate'
My path is not as yours
Our conversations as you know
Have opened many doors
So I will keep on keeping on
Whilst you're on level 2
And work to find my own true self
Though this seems hard to do
I know one day I'll find the truth
My heart will be wide open
And the bonds which binds us all
Will not be ever broken
Love Mum xxxx

Having replied to my mother's email, I switched off the computer knowing that it would be for the last time. As it was shutting down I sat in the large comfy chair and thought back through the day with a smile. I opened my notebook and wrote:

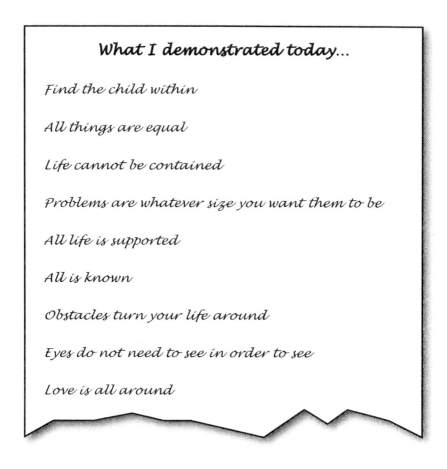

What I demonstrated today...

Find the child within

All things are equal

Life cannot be contained

Problems are whatever size you want them to be

All life is supported

All is known

Obstacles turn your life around

Eyes do not need to see in order to see

Love is all around

Chapter 5

KNOCKING ON HEAVEN'S DOOR?

Having sorted out the few bits and pieces which I needed to get rid of, the house was now ready for someone else to occupy. I was about to leave it for good, yet it was such a lovely sunny day that I decided to sit in the garden for a while. I reasoned with myself that to just sit and chill out for a while was still a part of my development on level 2. The ability to do nothing is often hard to achieve, so I thought I would give it a go!

The sun was shining down on me as I sat on the reclining garden chair. All was peaceful, a gentle cool breeze was blowing across my face, and in the distance I could hear the faint sound of a tractor gathering the final harvest of the season; winter was soon approaching.

I could feel my eyes becoming heavy and I began to drift into a sleep. This was unusual for me because since qualifying I found that sleep was very rare. I soon discovered that I didn't need as much sleep as I had once thought. In the past I needed to sleep not because I had done something, but because I had not done something. Anyway, I fell asleep on the recliner, I am not sure for how long, but it only seemed like a moment when my sleep was interrupted by the sound of footsteps walking across the gravelled drive.

As I was coming to, through blurry eyes I could see a figure walking towards me. I sat bolt upright, quickly tried to compose myself and pretended to be wide awake. As the person approached me I had to rub my eyes to make sure I was not dreaming. It was The Barefoot Indian.

"What are you doing here?" I asked in surprise and then bombarded her with questions. "Have I passed the task already?

Have you come to tell me I can go home?"

She didn't answer me and I guessed from the lack of response that her visit was not to tell me that I had passed level 2.

She stood smiling at me for a moment and then said, "I thought I would pay you a visit. I wanted to see how you were getting on, to see how you are."

"I'm fine." I said excitedly. "I can't believe you are here!"

I pulled out a chair for her to sit next to me. She looked stunning, more beautiful than I had ever seen her, if that was possible. She was breathtaking.

"You look fabulous!" I declared.

"You don't look too bad yourself," she said laughing.

I was delighted and thrilled that she was in my presence. It was like déjà vu, it was like old times and I secretly hoped that she would be staying with me for the duration of my task.

"What have you been up to?" I asked still in shock that my guru, my teacher, my friend, had decided to visit me.

"Well as you know I am now on level 3, which, I may add, is going very well," she replied.

"What is level 3 like?" I jumped in excitedly.

"All I can say about it is that you haven't seen anything yet!" she said, "But you will embark upon it soon enough. In the meantime you have to get through level 2. How are you finding it?"

"Not that bad at all, I found that level 1 was harder, level 2 by comparison is a breeze. I am just putting everything into practise really. Mostly I do this on my own though. I have met quite a few people along the way and guided them to entertain the possibility that there is another way and lightened their burden a little, but I have not met a particular individual who I can stay with like you did with me."

"That's Ok, each to his own way!" she declared. "Anyway it is not about others, it is all about you. All that's required of you is to demonstrate the love and compassion that is your true self, to never deny that which you are, to never hide the light that you are, to always be on show for all to see, and in doing this, you see and learn more about yourself than ever before."

"Yes, I can understand that," I said, thinking about what she had said.

She continued, "I have known others to pass level 2 without ever speaking a word or even seeing another person, or more to the point, without another person seeing them. In fact sometimes that can be the best way."

"Why?" I questioned.

"Well, it has happened on occasions that when embarking on level 2 a student can be so excited, eager to progress and to share all their knowledge, that they demonstrate to the world some of the miracles of life, you know the ones; walking on water, healing, being in two places at the same time and so on. They just want another person to understand the true potential of life, to see life as it really is and not to continue in a dream-like state full of suffering. But unfortunately their words and actions are misunderstood and suddenly they are seen as the miracle worker, the saviour, the problem sorter and soon the students are hounded by people wanting them to sort their lives out. Yet never once do those people take responsibility for their own lives and recognize that every-thing they witness they can do also. Suddenly the student has a following, but of course it is for all the wrong reasons."

Suddenly she stopped talking for a moment and then said, "Would you like me to show you what I mean?"

"Yes please," I said, "but how?"

"I shall show you how another one of my ex-students is getting on at the moment," she said.

"What other student?" I questioned.

"Well, when I was your training coach, you must have noticed that I was not always available or when I was with you I would suddenly have to leave?" she said.

"Yes, I remember, I would often wonder where you had to go in such a hurry."

"I was off to my other students who were on level1," she said. "I had five of you on the go all at once."

"Really!" I exclaimed. "How fascinating. Did we all pass?"

"Of course," she said smugly.

"Where are all the others now? What are they doing?" I asked eagerly.

"Some have just passed Level 2, however, there are a couple of them still here," she said. "I'll take you to one of them now."

"Great!" I said. "That will be fantastic."

"Come on then, let's go and meet him," she said.

She stood up and took hold of my hand and in the next moment we were standing in a palatial room surrounded by art on the walls and antique furniture which filled the room. I glanced around at the surroundings and couldn't help but think how immaculate everything looked.

The Barefoot Indian made herself comfortable on a velvety sofa. I continued to pan the room when suddenly I heard the door opening. In walked a man who was tall and slender, with the ageless quality about him that was now so familiar to me.

"Hello!" he exclaimed in an excited voice, whilst walking towards The Barefoot Indian. "I am so pleased to see you. I have been waiting for you."

'Why had he been waiting for her?' I wondered to myself, not that it mattered. Anyway, they progressed with their greetings and after a short while she introduced him to me, we soon got chatting and compared stories about our adventures. After talking and laughing for some time, my attention was drawn back to the room in which were sitting. I suddenly said to him, "What a beautiful house you live in, the way you have dressed this room is very peaceful and calming."

"It needs to be!" he exclaimed. "My house is like a retreat; a place for me to get away from it all."

"What do you mean?" I enquired. "What do you need to get away from?"

"Just wander over to that window and have a look outside," he said pointing to the large sash window. "I think you will have your question answered."

I moved over to the window and looked through it.

"Oh my God!" I shouted in surprise.

I couldn't quite believe what I was seeing for in front of the house stood a crowd of people, let me rephrase that, in front of the house stood a mass of people. It was like looking at a crowd at a pop concert and some were even waving banners. I glanced at some of the signs and these were just a few of what I saw *'Please heal me next' 'What are the winning lotto numbers?' 'Make my boss a nicer person' 'Where is my soul mate?"* Having read enough I turned away from the window.

"Oops," I said, "it seems like you are going to be busy."

"I know," he said, shaking his head in despair. He then proceeded into what I can only describe as a rant."I just can't seem to get the message through to those people outside that I am not a problem solver, but that I am like a mirror reflecting to them their own capabilities, reflecting their own sovereignty. With every action they take in their lives and with every word that comes out of their mouths, they give away their own power, they surrender their own will for another's, and in doing so they live their lives in emotional poverty and fear. Why can't they understand that it is so difficult, if not impossible, to win the lotto and buy the house of their dreams and yet it is so easy to manifest the house of their dreams by simply knowing the genius, the supreme intelligence, that created it? Why do they search for the perfect partner whilst never once striving to be perfect themselves? Why do they claim they want world peace when all they really want is inner peace, which is easier to achieve? Why do they take pride in judging others and then act surprised and angry when they are judged? Why do they punish a wrong doer when the act of punishment itself makes them a wrong doer?..." And on and on he went.

Finally, after what seemed like an eternity he fell silent. The Barefoot Indian and I both felt relieved when he stopped talking. He then suddenly turned to me and asked

"What would you do if you were in my situation?"

"Erm... Let me think about that one for a moment," I replied slightly taken aback.

We sat in silence as I pondered his question and then I progressed with answering it.

"Firstly," I said, "I would like to say that I am glad that I am not in your situation, though, if I were, this is what I would probably do...

"I would write a note and pin it to the front door which says *'Out to lunch! But should you wish to Know thyself enter here. All are welcome. This door is never locked.'* Then I would sit back, relax and wait for those who entered."

"Brilliant!" he exclaimed excitedly. "That may whittle down the workload!"

"It may do," I said, "but maybe they will all enter!"

"Well," he said, "whichever way it goes my father's house is big enough and if they all decide to enter at least they have shown a willingness to listen; to come to some understanding."

He stood up and walked over towards a desk at the far end of the room.

"I shall just grab some paper and a pen and get the sign written. The sooner I pin it to the door the sooner I can be off."

What did he mean by the sooner I can be off? I wondered to myself.

When he had finished writing out the sign he turned to The Barefoot Indian and said,

"I'll just go and attach this to the door and then we can make a move."

He left the room quickly.

"What does he mean 'make a move?" I asked her in an alarmed tone.

"Ah, yes, I forgot to mention that he has already successfully completed Level 2 and will be heading back to Head Office with me."

"But what about all those people outside?" I enquired nervously.

"You seem to have that in hand. Your suggestion makes perfect sense and I am sure you will handle any visitors through the door with ease," she replied in her usual knowing tone.

"But...But..." I stumbled. I fell silent and thought about what had just occurred. When I had recovered my composure I continued, "I get the feeling that I have been set up."

"I suppose in a way you have," she said smiling. "It is all part of your learning. Everything is set up for you to be able to delve deeper into your boundless wisdom. Nothing happens by chance. We thought you could benefit from a little push, just to speed things up a bit. We knew you would not have come here today if I had told you what was in store for you!"

"Well that's true!" I said and then in a resigned voice I added, "Very well, I shall do the best I can."

"That is all you can ever do," she laughed compassionately.

Having pinned the note to the door, the two of them were preparing to leave for Head Office. Oh, how I envied them, though in a loving way. I knew I was to remain here to fulfil my destiny and it was only a matter of time before I would be joining them again. I congratulated him for passing level 2 and we said our goodbyes. As quick as a flash they were gone.

So here I was, not quite sure what to do next, in this rambling, palatial house with a mass of people outside. I sat for a while in the silence before moving to the window once again to take a look outside. The people were still there, but were now forming a queue as they read the sign on the door. As yet no one had entered. I decided to draw the curtains to close out the crowd and bring the day to an end. 'Tomorrow is another day,' I thought to myself, 'for now I just want to sit and meditate on the events of the day.'

As I sat in luxury thinking about the clever way The Barefoot Indian had set me up, my cell phone went off and interrupted my thoughts.

Message from Head Office:
You are doing so very well. Just a little reminder for you

Whatever you have in your mind - forget it
Whatever you have in your hands - give it
Whatever is to be your fate - face it!

We also thought you would appreciate the following joke following today's events!
Man - what is a million years like to you?
God - like one second
Man - what is a million dollars like?
God - like one cent
Man - can I have a cent?
God - just a second!

Alw n r thoughts xxx

When I had finished chuckling at the text message, I decided to explore the rest of the house, which I suddenly found myself occupying. It was a very large, rambling, opulent house and each room was furnished beautifully. Any house that has 'Court' in the title gives you some idea of how stately this house was, and you could tell from the portraits hanging on the wall that the house had been in the same family for generations and history oozed from every corner.

'There are worse places to stay, I suppose,' I thought to myself sarcastically as I wandered around. 'I just have to deal with the mass of people that are waiting outside.'

After a while, though, as I was settling in to my new abode the thought of the crowds outside didn't seem to be so bad. After all, life was for exploring new opportunities and as Head Office reminded me *'Whatever is to be your fate – face it!'*

Whilst I was waiting for the next day to arrive, I tried again to change the ring tone on my cell phone, but to no avail. In frustration I gave up and turned my attention to my notebook and wrote the following:

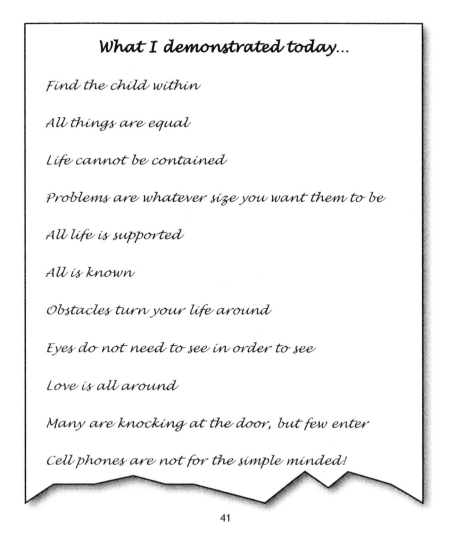

What I demonstrated today...

Find the child within

All things are equal

Life cannot be contained

Problems are whatever size you want them to be

All life is supported

All is known

Obstacles turn your life around

Eyes do not need to see in order to see

Love is all around

Many are knocking at the door, but few enter

Cell phones are not for the simple minded!

Chapter 6

SOUP–REME BEING?

The next morning I pulled back the curtains to see what was happening with the crowd of people waiting outside, but it was still too dark to see anything. I knew that no one had come through the door, so they must all still be waiting outside, but maybe a few had gone home.

The sun was just beginning to rise and as always I felt compelled to watch it. As the sun began to dawn, you could tell from the colors in the sky that today was going to be a cold and frosty one. 'Those poor people out there must be frozen, I must offer them some soup,' I thought to myself. No sooner had I had thought this than my mind suddenly took off, it was like a light bulb had been switched on in my head. What started out as a small thought of generosity soon turned into a full scale production...

'What a great idea! I shall give them soup. That would be a perfect demonstration of the 'Unlimited',' my thoughts continued... 'to feed all those people out of thin air would surely get them thinking, but how would I do it? ... I know! I could take out a thermos flask of soup maybe a litre in size and then let gallons and gallons of soup keep pouring from it like a never ending river of soup! I could occasionally change the flavor, I could have a basket of bread rolls and every time one was taken out another would magically replace it. Brilliant! That is what I will do. It is bound to get their attention, surely they will want to know how it's done? They will want to know the boundless, magnificent 'Unlimited' force that makes all things possible.'

I was suddenly filled with excitement and eagerness as I planned my demonstration, at last I was ready to face my destiny, ready to fulfil my fate.

Thoughts were swimming around in my head and expanding in all directions as I made my way to the kitchen to make the first batch of soup. When the soup was ready I placed some bread rolls in a rustic wicker basket that I found in the larder and placed everything on the kitchen table ready to take outside when the moment came. Eagerly I made my way back to the room to take a look outside at the waiting crowd. I entered the room filled with thoughts of excitement, but then in one single moment they came crashing to a halt, like the slamming of the brakes in a car when you do an emergency stop. The sun had risen enough to shed light on the grounds outside. Not one person was standing there.

'Where have they all gone?' I wondered. I strained my head to glance around the grounds from the window, yet there was not a solitary soul in sight. I wasn't sure whether I felt relieved or disappointed.

I stood by the window for a short while wondering why everyone had decided to go home and felt disappointed for them that they had missed the opportunity to witness the 'Unlimited' at work.

I was just contemplating my next move when I heard a faint voice calling out. It seemed to be coming from the hallway. "Hello," the voice said. "Hello, is anybody here?"

I went to investigate. To my surprise there were seven people standing in the hallway.

"Hello," I said greeting them, "Can I help you?"

"I hope so," said a young woman on behalf of the group. "We saw the sign on the door and felt compelled to come in. So here we are!"

"Fantastic." I said as a new wave of excitement came over me. "Please come through and make yourselves at home."

I led them from the hallway into the a large comfy sitting room. As they were making themselves comfortable, I suddenly remembered the soup. 'Here was my chance, my opportunity,' I thought.

"Would anyone like some hot soup with rolls?" I asked. "You must be cold, it will warm you up."

"No thank you," they said, almost in unison.

"Are you sure?" I enquired almost pleading.

"Positive, thank you," was the reply.

'Will I ever get to demonstrate my eternal soup?' I thought to myself.

When they were all sitting comfortably and chatting amongst themselves, it became apparent to me that they had only just met one another and the sign on the door had brought them all together. There was a sense of curiosity mixed with uncertainty in the atmosphere and I got the feeling that the sooner I said something, the better it would be for all of them.

"Why did you come through the door?" I suddenly asked.

They turned to look at one another as if waiting for someone to speak first, each looking slightly nervous. Soon a middle-aged man nervously began to talk.

"I am not quite sure why I came in through the door, but I think it is down to the fact that I have had a yearning all of my life for something, yet without ever really knowing what I was yearning for. I've tried to fulfil the yearning with all sorts of things; relationships, money, work, the usual stuff, but I am still yearning. Life has always been a mystery to me. I have always felt that something was missing and because of that I find my life so tiresome! I saw the note on the door and suddenly felt moved to enter, so I came in. I have nothing to lose by doing so, so here I am."

The others in the room were in general agreement with what the man had said.

"Great!" I exclaimed. "Now that you are here, let's begin."

As I glanced around the room, it reminded me of a small classroom filled with children on their first day of school, though, rather than them all being of the same age, it was mixed, ranging from about 23 to 85 and from all different types of backgrounds. Some of them proceeded to take out a notebook and pen, ready and eager to write in a studious kind of way. I was just about to speak when a lady put her hand up in the air, just like a child does when they want permission to speak. I smiled to myself.

"I am presuming that this is some sort of lesson on enlightenment, if I am correct then should we not sit in a particular way?" she asked.

"What do you mean?" I asked her.

"Well, I thought maybe we should be sitting crossed-legged on the floor or something." she replied.

"That won't be necessary," I said smiling. "To be enlightened is to be free from all restrictions which includes pain. Your body is already burdened, you do not need to add to this by sitting in a way that is uncomfortable and unnatural to you, but if it is comfortable for you to sit that way then please, feel free to do so."

Their faces seemed to lighten up at my words and they began to relax. Those with notebooks and pens began to scribble down what I had said. I couldn't get the image of the classroom out of my mind so I decided to begin with that.

"Let's start the first lesson of the day." I said. " What is the answer to this simple sum, one plus one equals…?"

They looked at me in a surprised way, as if I was mad or something, but this didn't bother me and I waited for them to answer. One chap suddenly said, "Are you serious, do you really want us to answer that?"

"Of course." I replied and then repeated the question, "What does one plus one equal?"

In unison they all shouted "Two!"

"Wrong answer!" I replied. "The correct answer is one plus one equals one!"

Their faces were perplexed.

"If there is one thing you need to know above everything else it is this," I said, and then continued, "If you add two things together and you say they are different, then one plus one equals two, but if you say that the two things you are adding together are one, and the same one, then one plus one equals one."

The perplexed expressions on their faces had now turned into a blank vacant look. I smiled to myself for I knew that this simple sum, one day, would make perfect sense. It is inevitable, just like the inevitability of an apple falling from a tree when it is ripe, it falls in a single moment. In the same way enlightenment will come, it is the only thing that will ever come.

I carried on, "You need to seek out the one, the one that is in all things and is all things. On discovering this, everything will add up, all will make sense."

A member of the group raised their hand to speak and said, "But how do we find the one? Where do we begin?"

"You have already started, but whether you have realized this or not is another matter," I answered. "Your life so far, indeed many lifetimes so far, has been rather like doing a jigsaw puzzle. You have been putting the pieces together little by little. As the picture begins to emerge and the puzzle is nearing completion, you begin to see that one piece is missing, and it is that piece, that is the one, that is the most crucial, for without it the picture is not complete and never will be. But you will only find the last piece, the one, when all the other pieces have been put together. When it is found and you finally place the last piece lovingly amongst all the other pieces, the picture is then complete, your task will be done."

I went on, "You walked through the door today because the puzzle is nearing completion and you are beginning to realize that the one piece is missing and it is that one piece that you yearn to find."

Again some of them were scribbling away in their notebooks.

"To complete the picture, the puzzle, you will need the following – patience, tolerance, commitment, the ability to work alone, but above all you will need a sharp eye, you will need to be at your most observant."

The room was silent as they took in my words. I gave them a few moments to reflect on the philosophy before interrupting the silence.

"Well, that's the technical bit over with, let's do some practical stuff."

Those that were writing suddenly stopped and the group sat up straight as though eager to continue.

I handed out a piece of paper to them all and as I was doing so I asked them to write down all the miracles they had witnessed in the last week.

"I shall give you about an hour, which should be plenty of time," I said.

"That's more than enough time for me," one of them said, "I think one minute would be enough time, I've never seen a miracle!"

The room was filled with mirth as they all burst out laughing as though in agreement with this.

"Well, try and think very hard over the past week, you may be surprised," I said in response.

"Why are we doing this?" one of them asked.

"It gives us all some idea of where your attention is, but more importantly where it ought to be," I said seriously.

I left them to it, but to be honest I didn't see much activity in the writing department! When the hour was up I collected the papers from them. I sat quietly while I looked through them, the group sat waiting and awkwardness filled the air. Every page was blank apart from their names written at the top. After some moments a voice broke the silence.

"How well did we do?"

"You did very well, it's exactly as I expected, you are in total denial of what's all around you. You are totally blind," I said laughing.

The group shuffled in embarrassment.

"But that's good, now that you acknowledge that, you can now pay attention, you can now begin to see."

A woman interrupted me. "What should we have seen? Can I ask what miracles did you see in the last week?"

"Well," I began, "in the last week I saw the moon and stars suspended in the heavens, twinkling brightly like jewels in God's crown; I saw every living thing breathing with the breath of life; I saw birds soaring in freedom; I saw the sun rise and set each day and as it did, it displayed the most colourful picture on a vast canvas called the sky. I felt the planet spinning like a Christmas bauble on a branch of the universe. I heard the sound of laughter and of crying and I knew that when I heard this, God was alive. I witnessed the rain washing the world clean. I watched nature preparing to settle down to lie dormant for the winter. I observed the mountains standing proud, omnipresent, unmoveable. I felt the wind brush my face and smiled as it swept away my yesterdays, making way for my tomorrows," I paused. "Shall I go on?"

They shook their heads in acknowledgement that I had made my point.

"So you see, miracles are everywhere, you just need to open your eyes and see. Pay attention, stop walking around in a dream-like state. Remember you need to be alert to find the missing piece."

The room was silent and the group was in deep contemplation. I walked around the room handed them another piece of blank paper and suggested that from this day forward they write down all the miracles that come their way. Suddenly the 85-year-old put his hand up in the air, wishing to say something.

"Before you speak," I said to him, "I would like to ask you a question first. Why did you put your hand up in the air? Why did you not just say what you wanted say?"

"I guess it's a habit that has been with me since I was a child," he replied sheepishly. "It's a way of asking for permission to speak."

"How many of you in the room agrees with this?" I asked.

With that every hand went straight up in the air and I could not help but giggle.

"Let me show you something," I said to the 'class'. "If you would all like to come over to the window."

They all proceeded over to the large sash window and just as I had anticipated, a large bird was circling above the manicured grounds.

"I want you to watch the bird for a while," I said and as perfect students, they did so.

A short while later the bird swooped down and landed gracefully on a patch of grass to the side of a herbaceous border. I turned to them and asked.

"Who gave the bird permission to land there?"

They thought about this for a short while before one of them answered

"No one gave it permission to land."

"Why not?" I asked.

The 'class' was silent as they pondered this. The 85-year-old broke the silence.

"I suppose there isn't anything that can give the bird permission to land. It just lands where it wants to."

"Why is that?" I asked him.

"Well, I guess it's free, nothing has control over it, it can go wherever it chooses and it can do whatever it desires. It just seems to be that way!"

"So what makes you different?" I asked. "Who do you need to seek permission from?"

I continued, "Look around you, all the clues are there, nature reflects your true self. There is no one and nothing that can give permission to the bird and so it is with you. All life is equal. What is true for the bird is true for you also. Be like the bird. Only in your mind does the difference appear. If you are seeking permission for something, you are going to be waiting a very long time!"

"So are you saying that we can do whatever we want to do?" one of them asked.

"I am saying that you are free to be," I replied.

After a short pause, I concluded, "I guess you have just witnessed your first miracle."

They continued to watch the bird, while contemplating what they had just heard. Eventually I interrupted the silence by asking the 85-year-old, "Now what was it you wanted to ask me?"

"I can't remember, it couldn't have been important," he replied, shaking his head.

As one by one they moved away from the window I suddenly remembered the soup.

"Would anybody like some soup now? I asked.

Again they said no.

I could tell from their faces that they were all deep in thought and food was the last thing on their minds. I suggested we called it a day. They had a lot to think about.

"I hope you have enjoyed your first day," I said. "We should all get together again in the morning. In the mean time, contemplate what you have heard today."

"We certainly will!" said one of them, "but is that it for today? Can't we do more? It has been so enlightening, I would like to continue."

"Enlightenment comes in small doses otherwise it would be overwhelming," I said smiling. "To gain wisdom you have to strip away the layers of misconceptions. It is like peeling an onion, each layer has to be removed slowly until eventually you get to the centre, the source. But rest assured, you will get there," I said.

"But before you go, there is something I would like to say. If you do decide to come back tomorrow, please consider this: You will be embarking upon a journey, yet the destination will be unclear. There are no rules, there are no methods, there are no techniques, there are no tools. Although you will be in a group, you will walk alone. I may show you many things, but it is down to you to see them. I may say many things, but it is down to you to hear them. I can only point out to you a direction, but it is down to you to follow it. There is only one way to self discovery and that is through self."

With that they all reluctantly left to go home.

When they had gone I decided to have the soup myself. I poured it from the thermos flask and proceeded to devour it. It was divine. At least I got to enjoy it!

As I was soaking up the last dregs of the soup with my bread roll, I could hear my cell phone ringing from deep within my handbag. I quickly pulled it out, not because I was eager to read the message, but I was keen to stop it ringing!

Message from Head Office:

Well what can we say!
Those who really seek the path to enlightenment dictate terms to their minds. Then they proceed with strong determination.
The greatest gift is to give people your enlightenment, to share it. It has to be the greatest.
Peace b w/u alw xxx

That evening I sat in the sitting room with my feet up and decided to do something that I had not done for such a long time – watch the television. Although I was watching it, my mind kept wandering through the events of the day and I wondered if the 'class' would return in the morning. When the news came on I decided to write in my notebook whilst everything was still fresh in my mind.

What I demonstrated today...

Find the child within

All things are equal

Life cannot be contained

Problems are whatever size you want them to be

All life is supported

All is known

Obstacles turn your life around

Eyes do not need to see in order to see

Love is all around

Many are knocking at the door, but few enter

Cell phones are not for the simple minded!

The world is like a classroom

There is only 'one'

Miracles are everywhere

All life is free to be

The only permission to seek is that of your own

I can make soup!

Chapter 7

END OF TERM

The 'students' did turn up the following day and the next and the next. Not only did they turn up, but each one brought with them more people. The class was growing daily. As the days and months went flying by we spent many hours learning, exploring and expanding, but above all we were having fun. To put together the jigsaw puzzle is not meant to be a chore, once you realize the objective and understand that is your goal then you can progress with optimism and clarity. Yes, there are times when you feel that you are not getting anywhere and everything is against you and of course there will be times of frustration, doubt and anguish, however, in these moments it only goes to demonstrate your willingness to complete the puzzle and to see the whole picture.

The students' eagerness and willingness increased with each day and I could see each one of them blossoming and growing into their own unique natural being. As they began to explore their own fears, motives and expectations, they soon recognized that all of those thoughts had no more power over them than shadows have that are cast by the sun. You can only see a shadow when you are turned away from the sun, with the light behind you.

The students were turning to face the light and it showed. Gone was the anguish from their faces and the worries that they carried around with them from day to day like rubbish sacks, they were becoming light and free. They were like butterflies emerging from their cocoons and it was when I saw this that I realized they no longer required me, they were ready to go it alone.

When everyone was gathered I announced: "You are now

ready to go it alone."

I paused before adding, "Your time here with me has come to an end."

Silence filled the air, you could have heard a pin drop. I glanced around the room and saw a slight panic emerging on their faces.

"What are you worried about?" I asked.

After another silent moment one of the women spoke. "Well," she mumbled, trying to find the right words, "I think we have become a little complacent. There is a sense of security knowing that you are here to point us in the right direction."

"Yes, I can understand that," I said, "but the greatest gift I can give you now is to let you go, you need to keep discerning more of yourselves each day and only you can do that. There is no more you need from me, in truth you never needed me, you have all that you need with you. Always!"

I continued, "I want you to see that all is possible because of who and what you are. You have spent so long believing that your salvation lies in something other than yourself, when in truth only you and you alone can set yourself free."

I looked around the room and noticed that the panic on their faces was turning into a resigned look. A man sitting at the far end of the room suddenly spoke. "Is this our last day with you?"

I looked again at their faces and being the compassionate big softie that I am I reckoned there would be no harm in squeezing in another day. "Let's make tomorrow the last day." I said. "Let's make our final hours together the most memorable yet!"

Suddenly a sense of excitement filled the air and all thoughts of the future seemed to disappear from their minds.

"Right." I said. "Let's begin! This morning I want you all to go out and about. Have no thought of where you are going, just start walking, see where the 'Unlimited' takes you. Pay attention to its voice within your heart, let it speak, let it guide you. Be unlimited. Whatever comes your way, embrace it, for whatever comes your way is a gift and as with any gift you have to carefully unwrap it, peel away the packaging. Only by stripping away the wrapping paper can you see what is there. I want you to pay particular attention to how much you resist saying what it is you really want to say. How many times have you felt the words arising from your heart, yet, through fear, you deny saying them and continue to speak in a way that you assume is acceptable to those around you?"

"I do that all the time!" exclaimed one of the women. "I want to say one thing, but I push that aside and say what I think the person would like to hear!"

"Well now's the time to say only what you want to say, say what is in your heart." I then continued. "Should you complete this little task today, perhaps you would like to come back here later, so that we can compare notes."

When I had finished speaking, I was bombarded with questions. Their fear of the unknown had suddenly risen to the surface (which I have to add is always a good thing). To ease their anguish I suggested they consider the following:

"A piece of drifting wood has no choice than to place all of its trust in the ocean, for it is the ocean that is carrying it to its destination. You must be like the drift wood, place all of your trust in the ocean of life for it knows where your destination lies."

With some reluctance the room began to empty as they began their mission for the day. When the last one had left, the room felt strangely quiet and a slight tinge of disappointment came over me as I knew this chapter of my life was coming to an end and as yet I was unaware of what was to come next. Maybe I am nearing the completion of Level 2, I suddenly thought to myself, perhaps I will soon be returning to Head Office. Suddenly my heart filled with excitement and I pondered for a while about my return.

I decided to take a walk in the magnificent grounds of this beautiful house. As I prepared to go outside I couldn't help but think how lucky I was to end up staying in such a marvellous place, but my thoughts brought me back to reality. Of course it's not luck, it just demonstrates that whenever you give, you receive much more in return.

It was such a lovely calm sunny day, spring had arrived and the air was filled with a fresh, crisp smell. I breathed deeply, filled my lungs and soaked in the peaceful atmosphere as I made my way towards the summer house across the manicured lawns. As I approached it I noticed to the right of me, in the distance, one of the students staring gloomily into the large pond, or maybe I should say a small lake. Anyway, he looked despondent so I decided to investigate.

"What's wrong?" I asked as I approached him.

He turned to look at me with sad puppy dog eyes.

"I don't think I am capable of knowing the 'Unlimited'. I find it so difficult," he said. "Everyone has gone off, following their hearts, following the 'Unlimited' and here I am, Mr pathetic. I couldn't travel more than a hundred yards. How limited am I?"

I couldn't help but smile to myself as I listened to him.

"Why do you assume that because you have traveled a couple of hundred yards that you are limited?" I said. "Perhaps you are exactly where you are meant to be."

"Well I'm not exactly going to see much here am I?" he said looking at me again with those sad eyes.

"There's nothing here except a pond and how could I possibly learn anything from that!" He exclaimed.

"That is down to you," I replied. "You have the opportunity to learn from anything, if you are willing."

He continued to sit and ponder on what I had just said. After a short while he turned to me and said, "I feel as though I am willing, but I can't see how the pond can teach me anything."

"You'd be surprised at what it can reveal to you," I said. "The pond can show you exactly what's going on within you and reveal to you your natural state."

"Really?" he said, suddenly excited. "How? I'd love to see

that!"

"Then you shall," I declared.

I made my way over to some large trees behind the summer house and hunted around for a couple of small fallen branches to use as sticks. When I had collected them I took them back to the pond and offered one of them to him.

"I want you to take this stick and along with me we are going to stir the water up as furiously and vigorously as we can," I said as he took the stick from me. "I shall tell you when to stop."

We made our way to the edge of the pond. The water was calm and peaceful.

"Are you ready?" I asked.

"Yep."

"OK, after three," I instructed, "One, two, three..."

We spent a good few minutes stirring up the water, it was only when my arms started to ache and sweat was pouring from his brow that I shouted "Stop!"

"Now, I want you to look at the water and describe to me what you see, describe what state the water is in?"

"It's in turmoil," he said, "it's all over the place, moving in different directions, it doesn't know what's hit it."

"Carry on," I instructed.

"Well, it looks angry, it looks upset, it's disturbed, it's scattered, it doesn't know what to do."

"OK," I interrupted. "That will do. What you have just described, does any of that sound familiar?"

He looked at me a bit puzzled, then after a few moments it suddenly dawned on him.

"It sounds like me! That's how I feel!"

"That's right, it does sound like you!" I said. "Now, just watch the water for a while."

He did this and when the water had calmed down and returned to the state it was in before we had stirred it up, I turned to him.

"What do you see now?" I questioned.

"Calmness, stillness, clarity, tranquillity, knowingness, certainty," he said. "It's at peace, shall I go on?"

"No, I think we get the picture," I replied and then asked, "Why did the pond return to that state after we stirred it up?"

He contemplated this for what seemed like an eternity and then suddenly said, "Because that is how it was before, it returned to its natural state."

"Excellent!" I exclaimed. "So if we stirred it up every day, would it make any difference?"

"No, it would always return to its natural state at some point," he replied.

"So no matter what we did or however hard we tried to alter the water, it would always return to that state of calmness?" I posed.

"Yes, always," he answered. "It can't be any other way."

"And so it is with you," I said. "No matter how much you get stirred up, no matter what you go through, you will always return to your natural state. The moment you decide to stop stirring yourself up and tiring yourself out in the process, you will experience what's always there. Peace is at hand, yet you keep disturbing it."

"Wow," he said, "I've never seen it like that before."

"I don't suppose you have," I said.

"All that wisdom from a little pond," he concluded.

We both laughed.

He picked up the stick again and began to gently stir the water then waited for it to calm down again. He repeated this for a while and I could see he was absorbing this universal truth.

I left him to it for a while, but then decided to give him a real treat as this was probably the last opportunity both of us would get.

"Would you like to see the 'Unlimited' in action?" I asked him.

"I would love to," he replied excitedly.

"Very well," I said. With that I turned my attention to the pond and it began to shake and ripple. To his amazement the water started to part. In moments the water had separated leaving a pathway for us to walk through. I grabbed his hand and led him through the walkway. His mouth was wide open and is eyes were nearly popping out of his head. When we reached the other side he was speechless. We climbed the bank and I got him to turn around to look back at the pond. It had returned to its natural state, calm, still and untouched.

"That was incredible," he finally said. " How was that done?"

"There is no 'how'. It is all very simple. The only thing that's required is for you to think with your heart not your mind. Whatever you can think within your heart is your will and thy will, will be done," I said. "This you will come to understand. Your mind will never grasp it, but your heart already knows."

He accepted my answer without question.

As we made our way back to the house he turned to me and said, "I have gained so much from today even though I got off to a rough start. Thank you."

"Now you can see that you were in the right place at the right time," I said, then continued, "You don't have to travel far to see wisdom, it is always at hand. Willingness to see is all that's required."

When we arrived back at the house we didn't have to wait too long before some of the others were starting to re-appear from their outings. I took a back seat as they began to compare the stories of their adventures and by the look on their faces I could tell that they had enjoyed and gained insight from the exercise. The rest of the day was spent chatting.

Eventually, as evening was approaching, I felt it was time to call it a day. They had a lot to contemplate as a result of their little adventure. It was when we were saying our goodbyes that I suddenly realized that a handful of students had not returned. Maybe they never will, I thought to myself, who knows where the

'Unlimited' has taken them?

It was such a lovely night that I spent the evening in the garden sipping a glass of wine and nibbling on some sandwiches. I observed my surroundings and marvelled at nature as it was busy settling down for the night, I soaked up the stillness of it all. Just as the light was disappearing I wrote in my notebook.

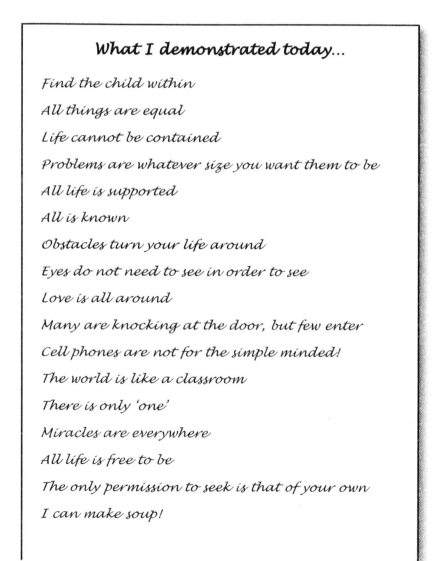

What I demonstrated today...

Find the child within

All things are equal

Life cannot be contained

Problems are whatever size you want them to be

All life is supported

All is known

Obstacles turn your life around

Eyes do not need to see in order to see

Love is all around

Many are knocking at the door, but few enter

Cell phones are not for the simple minded!

The world is like a classroom

There is only 'one'

Miracles are everywhere

All life is free to be

The only permission to seek is that of your own

I can make soup!

> *Give and you will receive*
>
> *To experience peace - stop disturbing it!*
>
> *The smallest thing can reveal the greatest thing*
>
> *The unalterable is unalterable*

No sooner had I finished writing than my cell phone began to ring, I knew it was a text from Head Office so I eagerly opened the message.

Message from Head Office:

All humanity by nature desire to know!
The things we tell of can never be found by seeking yet only seekers find it.
God bl$ xxx

How very true, I thought to myself, as I drank the last drop of Chardonnay.

Chapter 8

MASTER CLASS

Little did I know that when I pulled back the curtains on this morning that it would turn out to be the most extraordinary day, not just for the students, but for me also. It was after all the last day we would be spending together so I shouldn't have been surprised, but then sometimes you do forget to expect the unexpected!

The day started off as normal and after breakfast I still had plenty of time to spare before anyone was due to arrive. I was feeling very creative so I decided to produce a poster for all of the students which they could take away with them to use as a check list. It was a tool to keep them focused and to nudge them in the right direction.

I made my way over to the computer which sat on top of an antique desk in front of yet another large window. As I sat waiting for the computer to warm up, I glanced out of the window and noticed how foggy it was outside, the visibility was extremely poor and it was very difficult to see anything further than a few feet away.

Anyway, I progressed with what I was doing and ignored the gloomy weather. I sat down and began producing my poster. It came together very quickly as there were few instructions, yet they were all-encompassing. If any of them were to be acted upon, in any given situation, it would eventually lead to the destination.

Action Plan for Enlightenment

1. Acknowledge that we are all on the spiritual path. We never got on it and we can never get off it.
2. Make friends with wisdom. Endeavour to think like a wise person, strive to be wise. Ask yourself often 'is this what a wise person thinks and does?'
3. Know that your worries and anxieties have but a short time to live. They are like a bar of soap, at first it looks substantial, but it quickly diminishes and is destined to disappear.
4. Don't try to make things personal which are not personal to you. Ask yourself often 'what has this got to do with me?' Treat everything like a letter, check first that it is addressed to you.
5. Reserve judgment until you know what it is you are judging, because only then can your judgment be true.
6. Think of yourself as a gift to be given. Think only of giving, because only in giving can peace and contentment be found. Only through giving can you be aware of the one who gives.

As I was just finishing off and instructing the computer to print multiple copies, everything suddenly went dark, I could not see. It was as if someone had placed their hands over my eyes. They had!

"Jesus Christ!" I yelled in surprise and jumped slightly.

"Not quite, he's too busy," said a voice as he released his grip from my eyes. "I thought I would surprise you instead."

I turned around and to my delight there stood one of my colleagues from Head Office.

"What are you doing here?" I asked him excitedly. "Have you

come to tell me I can go back to Head Office, that I have successfully completed level 2?"

"No," he replied smiling, "although I have been watching
your progress when I have had the time."

"Why are you here then?" I asked hoping not to sound disappointed.

"Do I have to have a reason?" he enquired.

"Absolutely not!" I replied in a way that was obvious that I
was just pleased to see him."I am just curious, of all the people at
Head Office you would be the least likely person I would expect
to come here."

"Yes, you are probably right, but it is such a long time since I
have been here I was intrigued to see what it was like, to see how
things have changed – if at all," he said.

"Well, you certainly have dressed accordingly," I said
laughing as I looked him up and down. He was dressed head to
foot in designer gear, complete with Armani suit and Gucci shoes,
he looked immaculate, like a high flying entrepreneur.

"I like to make the effort," he said and then continued sardon-
ically, "one has to fit in. The fashion has certainly changed over
the centuries, the last time I was here the clothes were far more,
as they say, flowing," he said looking down at his attire.

"Yes, I suppose they were," I giggled.

I should at this point explain a little more about my colleague.
He was very rarely seen at Head Office, he would occasionally
pop in, but then he would be off again. You never questioned
where he was going or where he had been, you didn't need to,
you could tell just by looking into his eyes and experiencing his
presence that this guy was on a level way beyond my compre-
hension. The power that radiates from him is such that you feel
he could spin this planet on his little finger and toss it into orbit
(not that he ever would) and yet in the next moment he could pick
up something as small and delicate as a butterfly and mend its
broken wing by the gentle blow of his breath.

I have seen many awesome people in my time, however, this man is something else, forget about level 1,2,3,4… I long for the day when I am on his level! When you look into his eyes, it is like looking into the ocean, yet instead of seeing water you see a depth and a wisdom that goes on forever. His compassion, love and understanding is boundless and it radiates from every fiber of his being. I was so thrilled that he had decided to come and visit me.

"How long will you be staying?" I asked him once my excitement had began to wane.

"A few hours at the most," he replied. "I would like to meet your students, perhaps have a little chat with them and then I shall be off."

"That's fantastic!" I exclaimed. "They will be thrilled."

"Maybe, maybe not," he said in a matter of fact way. "It all depends on what they can see. Remember, I could stand amongst men for a thousand years and they would still be oblivious to what I am. They would delight in trying to ridicule me, persecute me and endeavour to knock me down. If they have one ounce of judgement in them they will not recognize me, if they are without judgement they will experience all that I am."

There was nothing I could add to this.

Shortly afterwards the students began to arrive, well the ones that were available, some had still not returned from their adventures from the previous day. As they began to pile into the large sitting room, they didn't seem to notice too much that we were joined by a new presence. They were used to people turning up out of the blue so one more didn't bother them and he certainly blended in even if he was a little too smartly dressed. Besides which, they were a little preoccupied with talking about the weather, for it truly was a dense fog and the fact that they had managed to get here was a miracle in itself.

When everyone was sitting comfortably and ready to progress with the final day, I walked around and began handing out my Action Plan for Enlightenment and as I was doing so I explained my reason for giving them this memo. They seemed genuinely pleased to receive it and I felt pleased with myself that I had gone to the effort of producing it. When they had finished absorbing the list my colleague stood up to address the room. He didn't introduce himself and there were no formalities; he just launched straight in.

"I think we should go outside."

The class looked at him in a bemused way, I am not sure if this was because he had suddenly started speaking to them or because of his suggestion to go outside on such a dreadful day. Anyway, without waiting for any response from them he was off out the door. With some hesitation they soon followed him.

We all stood with him on the manicured lawns, but to be honest the fog was so bad you could not really tell where you were standing, it was only the texture under our feet that gave us some clue.

"Now, I have brought you out here to show you something, or rather, for you to show me something," he began.

I looked at the students. Their faces were full of curiosity and I guess mine was too, and we all waited eagerly for him to continue.

"You have all been here many times and you should know these grounds like the back of your hand," he said and then continued, "I have a feeling that these grounds are quite magnificent. As this is my first visit here today and I can't see a thing due to the fog, I would appreciate it if you would help me in understanding what is here."

Without hesitation they individually began to describe to him what the grounds were like. As their descriptions progressed it became apparent to all of us that no two descriptions were the same, each description was different and yet they were all talking about the same place.

After some time when all had finished describing the scene, silence fell over them as they waited for him to speak.

"Thank you," he finally said, "but I am still no clearer as to what is here as all of your descriptions were different. Which one of you was telling the truth?"

No one answered him.

"Let me tell you who was telling the truth," he said smiling compassionately, "not one of you! All of you were describing to me your views, your opinions of what was here and as you can see, your opinions are not the same. Today you could not see the grounds, so you relied upon your memory, which, to be honest was a little unreliable and has distorted the truth."

The students were listening to him intently

"Your opinions are invisible to me they exist in your mind only, you can only ever describe them to me, but you can never show them to me."

They all nodded in agreement.

"You must be without opinions. Opinions blind you. The moment you judge something or have an opinion about something then that is all you can see, but only you can see it."

He fell silent for a short time and everyone was pondering his words when suddenly he asked, "Why did you not show me what was here?" He paused for a moment before asking, "Which is easier for you, to spend forever describing your opinions to me, which I can't see, or to simply show me what is visible to see?"

One of the women decided to answer. "I really want to say that it would be easier to show you what is visible, but on a day like today it is impossible because of the fog," she said in a concerned tone.

"Once you have seen what is here to see, without opinions and judgements, then there is nothing throughout eternity that can ever hide that. Not even fog!" he said.

The students were soaking up his words like a sponge, yet they had a perplexed look on their faces after his last comment. Their thoughts were suddenly interrupted when my colleague said, "Let me show you what I mean."

He turned around to face the grounds, his back was facing them. He stood motionless for a few moments and without saying a word, raised his arms into the air, clicked his fingers and what happened next, one can only marvel at. The fog instantly disappeared to reveal the most perfect garden. The light was dazzling, so bright that a few of the students reached for their sunglasses. The aromas wafting from the flowers were sublime, silence filled the air, peace radiated from every living thing and the colors were vibrant. I looked at the students, who were motionless and speechless as they took in the paradise that lay before them.

My colleague turned to them and said, "Today I have shown you what is here to see, why did you not do the same for me?"

Everyone remained silent, no one could answer him.

The silence was soon interrupted when a roebuck deer suddenly emerged from the bushes. It moved slowly forwards and was clearly in distress, it was limping on its fore leg and blood was trickling down to its hoof. The students saw the deer, but remained rooted to the spot knowing that any sudden movement would scare it away. We all observed the deer for a few moments then one of the students declared in a loud whisper, "The deer needs our help, it will never survive if we just leave it."

The other students were in agreement with this and began to discuss amongst themselves how they would go about helping it. "If we can manage to catch it, I have a friend who is a very good vet, he'll be able to help it, I'm sure."

Another said, "I know the owner of a nearby wildlife park, I am sure she would take it in and look after it. She has plenty of stables that she could put it in to help it recover and the staff are well trained to look after such animals."

Another suggested, "Maybe the wound is not as bad as it looks from here, let's try and catch it and have a look. If it's not too bad it will probably heal over in time. As they say, time is a great healer."

The students continued to come up with many possible plans

to help the deer, that's if they could catch it first. They were genuinely concerned for its welfare and all of them seemed to have a solution that they thought was best, they all knew of someone or something that could help it.

Suddenly, without any warning, my amazing, awesome friend put a stop to their plans. "Why don't you do something to help the deer?" he questioned them.

"That's what we are trying to work out," one of them answered.

"No you are not," he said. "You are trying to work out how to get someone else to sort out the problem, basically you are handing your problem over to someone else."

They all fell silent and again a quizzical look descended onto their faces. My friend continued, "You have all discussed the best way forward for the deer, but all of your suggestions have included another person. Take the vet for example, that's not you doing something for the deer, that is you getting someone else to do something for the deer. I even heard a suggestion to hand the deer over to time, that time is a great healer."

They all remained silent as they listened intently to him.

"Don't you see what you are doing?" he questioned, but did not wait for an answer. "You give power to all of those things which are not you – the vet, your friends, your family, the list goes on. You even claim that time itself has more power than you do. Which is easier for you, to work out who to hand the deer over to or for you to help the deer yourself, right here, right now?"

One of the younger students said, "I would like to say that it would be easier for me to help the deer, right here, right now, but I really don't feel I know what to do."

"That's because you are so used to relying on someone or something that you have never explored what you are capable of. Let me give you some clue as to your potential," he said as he made his way over to the deer.

To the students' surprise, as he began to walk towards the deer, the deer began to walk towards him. In no way was the deer timid or frightened, quite the opposite. When the two met, my colleague placed one hand on the deer's neck and the other on the deer's wounded leg. My colleague whispered something under his breath, but we couldn't hear what it was, in the next moment he released his hands and the wound had vanished. The deer, as quick as a flash spun around and ran off into the nearby trees, happy, content and apparently without pain.

"That's amazing," said the group almost in unison.

"That's the way it is," said my friend. "When you don't surrender what you have to others, you'll be surprised at what you can do."

The students were chatting excitedly amongst themselves and discussing what they had just witnessed. You could hear optimism in their voices. One by one they stood up and began to explore the grounds that they were seeing for the first time. I just took a back seat and watched them as they absorbed the surroundings, my colleague likewise did the same.

After some time my inspirational, omnipresent friend decided it was time for lunch.

"I think we should take a break and have some lunch," he cried out to them, "I am getting very hungry!"

The students on hearing him began to make their way back over to us.

"What is there to eat?" he asked them. "I'm starving, where can I get some food?"

One of the students kindly answered him. "I usually go to a small sandwich shop in the village, you're more than welcome to come with me."

Another jumped in, eager to please. "I go to the local café, great food, why don't you go there, I highly recommend it."

Another eagerly said, "There are always plenty of ingredients in the kitchen to make something, just help yourself."

The students continued with their suggestions when again my

colleague interrupted them. "Why don't you feed me?" he asked.

"Isn't that what we have offered to do?" one of them asked, puzzled.

"I'm afraid not," he said smiling. "All of your suggestions have directed me away from you. Going to a shop, going to the café, going to the kitchen and so on. Not one of you has offered to feed me."

The students fell silent and from the look on their faces you could tell it was beginning to dawn on them that a theme was beginning to emerge. They knew by now that there was nothing they needed to say. They waited for my colleague to continue.

"When you are asked to feed the hungry, this is what you should do," he said and then proceeded to walk over to the summer house.

He beckoned for us to follow him, which we did. When we arrived at the summer house he flung open the doors and to everyone's surprise, laid out on covered trestle tables was a feast fit for a king. One by one we entered the summer house and the students' eyes glanced over the food with mouths wide open, and it wasn't long before they all tucked in to the divine feast. As they savored each mouthful, not a word was spoken.

When lunch was over, we made our way back to the lawns and sat down. It wasn't long before my incredible friend began to speak. "The purpose of my visit today was to draw your attention to how impotent you think you are. Through habit, you have got so used to being powerless that you don't even recognize it," he continued, "But your imagined impotence couldn't be further from the truth.

"I don't expect you from this day forward to suddenly be enlightened and to demonstrate what you have witnessed today, but I do expect that from today you will be more vigilant to your own limitations and how you have got into the habit of denying your own being. You view yourself as nothing and yet see others as everything. Don't give away your integrity, no matter what happens in your life, step back and observe, seek to find your own resolution within."

He briefly fell silent before adding. "Before I depart, do any of you have any final questions?"

"Yes!" said one of them eagerly. "I have witnessed some incredible things whilst I have been here, miracles if you like, things seem to emerge from thin air. What you have demonstrated today seemed to be effortless to you, you made it look so easy. It appears that whenever you think of something it is so, but whenever I try and think of something I just get a headache! What I really want to know is how do you do miracles?"

"Interesting question," replied my colleague chuckling, "but unfortunately you are asking the wrong question. Do not concern yourself with the 'how', be only concerned with the 'what'. Seek to ask, 'what' makes miracles possible, that will yield you an answer." He continued, "To find answers, you've got to ask the right questions. The right questions are as important as the answers. I shall leave that with you to consider."

Another student, out of curiosity, took the opportunity to ask, "What did you whisper when you were with the deer?"

All of the students were listening intently for his answer as though that would give them a clue as to how he helped the deer. "Ah yes," he said as though he had suddenly remembered, "I said, I hope this works, especially as I have an audience!"

The students faces fell with disappointment, but soon turned into laughter when they realized that he was joking. After a few moments he shared with us what he had actually imparted.

"All that I am I give to you. That is what I said to the deer."

Again, all were silent as they contemplated his words. It wasn't long though, before everyone began to take the opportunity to ask him further questions knowing that this would probably be their last chance. Their thirst for wisdom was evident with every word that came out of their mouths.

Eventually, the session was concluded when my infinite,

bright, superb friend declared, "I must leave you now, however, don't forget what you have seen here today."

"I don't think that would be possible," said one of the students as she wiped a tear from her eye.

"And remember, I have not shown you the miracles today to show off my supernormal powers, that would make me no more than a magician. The true purpose is to free you from your suffering."

With that he started to walk across the lawn, away from us, then suddenly stopped in his tracks, turned back to face us and said, "When you look to the sky at night and see the stars shining brightly and you marvel at the incredible display of infinity, just consider this if only for a single moment. What do the stars see when they look back at you?"

He continued to walk away from us. My heart was yearning to run after him and go with him. I wanted to yell out 'take me with you', but I knew it was not meant to be, I had to restrain myself, my time was not yet.

We watched him fade into the distance and just before disappearing all together he raised his arms, clicked his fingers and the fog descended once again as quick as a curtain call in a theater and I was certain it was denser than before. Typical, I thought to myself, their sense of humor never changes!

I turned to the students, "Well, I guess that's it, there is no more for you here. All that you need you already have."

The students were in no way reluctant to leave, quite the opposite, they were full of optimism and eager to progress alone. As they were preparing to leave and we were saying our farewells for the very last time, one of the students out of the blue said to me, "We shall see you again.'

"Why do you say that?" I enquired.

"I don't know, I just said it!" she said. "The words arose from my heart."

I didn't question her any further .

When all of the students had gone, the house felt strangely quiet and empty, not because there was no one in it, but because I knew the time had come for me to leave it too. It was also my time to move on. I knew that this would be my last night in the house, therefore, I decided to hand the house over to one of the students who I knew would make good use of it.

I placed the keys in an envelope ready to post them off to him the next morning. I wasn't yet aware of where I was heading next, though this did not concern me, all would become clear. I relaxed for the rest of the day and pottered about and as I was doing so I went over the events of the day in my mind. This was soon interrupted by the annoying ring tone of my cell phone and once again, I was eager to stop the dreadful noise so I opened the text message.

Message from Head Office:

The students have made great progress. Their thinking has simplified. They have not gained knowledge, but are removing the knowledge that they thought they had.
The mind is not a vessel to be filled, but a fire to be kindled.
Well done U! xxx

Later that evening I decided that there was no point in adding anything to my notebook as technically I had not demonstrated anything that day, but then I had second thoughts.

What I demonstrated today...

Find the child within

All things are equal

Life cannot be contained

Problems are whatever size you want them to be

All life is supported

All is known

Obstacles turn you life around

Eyes do not need to see in order to see

Love is all around

Many are knocking at the door, but few enter

Cell phones are not for the simple minded!

The world is like a classroom

There is only 'one'

Miracles are everywhere

All life is free to be

The only permission to seek is that of your own

I can make soup!

Give and you will receive

To experience peace - stop disturbing it!

The smallest thing can reveal the greatest thing

The unalterable is unalterable

I have amazing friends

Chapter 9

LIFE'S A BEACH!

After leaving the mansion, I spent a lot of time traveling around and not really settling anywhere. I met quite a few people along the way and spent some time with them, but I had arrived at the point when I needed a holiday, I needed some 'me' time. I am sure Head Office would disagree with this, for when you are in constant touch with the source of all things, Isness, the 'I', every day is like a holiday, however, as I had yet to complete level 2 and there was no indication from Head Office that I was nearing completion, I thought what the heck, I shall have a break from exploring and demonstrating what I am and go into retreat for a while.

I thought about where I would like to go and I figured the best solution would be to find a nice quiet tropical island, the thought of lazing around on a beach and drinking cocktails would be paradise. So off I went in search of my own little corner of heaven.

Having found the perfect place, I did a little exploring of the island and then set about doing nothing. I found a beach that was deserted, the ocean was crystal clear with a hint of turquoise and the waves gently lapped against the shore. The sand was almost white, very fine and warm from the sun's rays. I placed my towel down on to it and sighed as I lay down and made myself comfortable.

'This is heaven,' I thought to myself, there was not a soul in sight, no interruptions, even my cell phone was quiet. I guess Head Office had come around to my way of thinking and appreciated the fact that I needed some peace. They seemed to be leaving me to it or it could have been due to the fact that I had played around with some buttons on my phone, as I was still trying to change the stupid ring tone, and I think I may have accidently pressed something that I shouldn't have!

Anyway, the sun was blazing hot, but the gentle breeze rolling in off the ocean was enough to cool me down. I closed my eyes and listened to the ocean ebbing and flowing. 'Heaven and earth would have to fall away before I move from this spot,' I thought to myself.

I must have been lying there for about thirty minutes when I suddenly sat upright.

"God I'm bored," I said out loud as I glanced around to see if anyone was about. I was bored, I needed a challenge, I needed to be out and about, demonstrating, being, loving, giving, not sitting on a beach secluded from the world. I needed to be immersed in the world.

As I sat there wondering what to do next my thoughts were interrupted by a faint buzzing sound. I looked around to see if I could spot a tropical insect, but to no avail. The buzzing continued to grow louder and then I suddenly noticed that my towel was vibrating. I gingerly lifted up my towel to see what creature lurked beneath. To my relief it was my cell phone, I must have accidently put it onto quiet mode, but at least, finally, I had got rid of that annoying tune. I opened the message.

Message from Head Office:

No one lights a lamp and puts it in a place where it will be hidden, or under a bowl. Instead he puts it on its stand, so that those who come in may see the light.
4ever yrz
JC xx

There was nothing I could add to that, I could only nod in

agreement, however, I decided to seize the opportunity and make contact with Head Office by replying to the message.

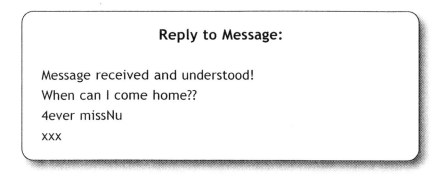

> ## Reply to Message:
>
> Message received and understood!
> When can I come home??
> 4ever missNu
> xxx

I waited eagerly for a reply, but it didn't come.

Realizing that to retreat was not for me, I gathered up all of my worldly belongings that I had with me at that time – a handbag and a towel (I like to travel light!) and set off once again into the unknown. I was not quite sure where to go or what to do so I just went with the flow and found myself strolling eastwards along the beach. I had been walking for only a short time when I was interrupted.

"Excuse me!" came a faint cry from behind me. "Excuse me!" the voice said again.

I turned around and saw a petite, tanned woman racing towards me, she was clearly trying to get my attention. I stopped in my tracks and waited for her to catch up with me.

"Hello," I greeted her as she approached me.

"Hi," she said slightly out of breath yet continued, "I'm sorry to trouble you, but I couldn't help noticing something quite extraordinary as you were walking."

"And what's that?" I enquired slightly surprised.

"I have been following you and as you walk you are not leaving behind any footprints in the sand!" she declared. "I can't quite believe it and I wouldn't if I had not seen it with my own eyes. Look," she said excitedly as she directed my attention to the sand, "there are only one set of footprints and they are mine."

Sure enough she was right. I hadn't noticed.

"What's going on?" she asked.

"I am light," I answered.

She looked me up and down and then said, "With respect, I think I am lighter than you."

I laughed at her misunderstanding. "You will come to understand what I mean when I say I am light," I said. "Just trust me, I am light."

She looked puzzled, so I continued, "I have no intentions of leaving my mark upon the world. I have no desire to impress."

"I don't understand," she said questioningly.

"Let me try to explain." I said. "This beach is like your life, the footprints you have left are merely impressions. Each day you strive to make a stamp upon the world, you long to let the world know that you are somebody, that you exist. You constantly impress your ideas onto others. Just like the footprints, you leave your mark, you want to be remembered. But let's look at the reality, the next person to come along this beach will see your footprints, your mark, yet what will their first thoughts be upon seeing them?"

She thought for a while.

"I guess it would be that someone has been here," she replied.

"And would they know who it was that had been here?" I asked.

"No."

"And what do the footprints tell them about you?" I asked.

She thought about this for a moment and then replied, "They tell them that I had come and gone."

"Anything else?" I asked, but I didn't give her time to answer."For example, would they know what an amazing person you were? Would they know how beautiful you are? Would they know how wise you are? Would they know all about your hopes and dreams?"

"No," she said, "they would know nothing about me."

"So, the only thing that your impressions say about you is that you have come and gone?" I questioned.

"Yes," she replied.

"What's the point of that?" I asked.

"There doesn't seem to be any point," she said in a matter of fact way.

"That's right, there is no point, so don't be concerned with impressions, or trying to impress, they say nothing about you."

"Yes, I can understand that," she said. "I have always been trying to leave an impression, to leave my mark and I guess from what I have just seen, that could be the reason why I always feel no one notices me."

We both fell silent for a moment and then I continued, "Only in your comings and goings do you leave a trail. Seek to find that which is ever present in the here and now. Find that and you will be immovable."

She stood motionless for ages whilst she thought about what I had said.

"One final thing," I said, interrupting her thoughts, "Where are your footprints now?"

She turned to look back over her trail just in time to see the last remaining footprints being washed away by the tide.

"You see, no matter how hard you try to leave an impression upon the world, they will disappear, they are only ever temporary and anything that is temporary is not real," I said. "Find that which is permanent."

She watched as her footprints disappeared.

"You have given me a lot to think about," she said.

"I am sure I have, but don't think too hard, the mind likes to complicate!" I said in response. "Let me show you how easy it is."

I picked up a stick that had been washed in by the tide and handed it to her.

"If you want to, write in the sand one thing that says the most about you, one thought that is with you every day."

She took the stick and without hesitation wrote *I am lonely.*

Within minutes the sea lapped in and washed her thought away.

"That's how flimsy your thoughts are, here one minute gone the next," I said. smiling at her. "You can write as many thoughts and feelings as you like, but they will all vanish at some point, so don't attach importance to them. Don't try to make permanent that which is so obviously temporary for they will all be washed away, in knowing that they will be washed away, you'll be less inclined to create them!"

She pondered this until I interrupted her again. "The only thing to be concerned with is what remained when the sea washed your thought away."

"What did remain?" she enquired.

"You tell me," I replied.

She thought long and hard before saying, "Well, I guess what remained was the one who wrote in the sand. Me!"

"So be it!" I said smiling and then added, "Ponder on what you have just said."

With that she began to write more of her thoughts in the sand and watched in relief as the ocean soon came and washed them away.

"It's like magic!" she declared excitedly.

"I suppose it is," I replied laughing, "your view of life is only an illusion built upon shifting sand. It will cave in."

She continued to write, in fact the beach was starting to look as though it had been hit by a graffiti artist. I decided to leave her to it.

"I have to go now," I shouted out to her as I began to walk away. "But I will see you again very soon."

She stopped what she was doing and made her way over to me. "I do hope we can meet again," she said.

"We will," I said. I still didn't know why I kept saying that to everyone I met.

"OK," she said, "But can I ask you one more thing?"

"Sure."

"I am standing right next to you, I have a shadow and you do not!" she said and then asked, "Why do you not cast a shadow?"

"I am light," I replied.

This time she did not respond as before, but softly said, "I guess you are," smiling whilst looking directly into my eyes.

"Never forget," I said, "a shadow can only exist when you obstruct the light. Remove the obstruction from your heart and there is only light. Let it flow."

With that we said our goodbyes and I left her on the beach whilst I continued my walk eastwards. Just before she disappeared from my sight all together I turned around and saw she was still writing in the sand and watching as the tide took them away. I giggled as I thought to myself how keen she was to be without all those thoughts and feelings that consumed her every day.

Not knowing where I was heading, I walked for ages. Eventually I sat down for a while on a large rock. The sunlight was starting to fade and a crescent moon was beginning to appear. Before continuing on with my adventure I took my notebook from my handbag and wrote:

What I demonstrated today...

Find the child within

All things are equal

Life cannot be contained

Problems are whatever size you want them to be

All life is supported

All is known

Obstacles turn your life around

Eyes do not need to see in order to see

Love is all around

Many are knocking at the door, but few enter

Cell phones are not for the simple minded!

The world is like a classroom

There is only 'one'

Miracles are everywhere

All life is free to be

The only permission to seek is that of your own

I can make soup!

Give and you will receive

To experience peace - stop disturbing it!

The smallest thing can reveal the greatest thing

The unalterable is unalterable

I have amazing friends

There is only light

Impressions do not impress

All thoughts are temporary

All emotions will be erased

As the light faded altogether, I was still waiting eagerly for Head Office to reply to my earlier text, but it never came.

Chapter 10

FLOWER POWER

Another encounter occurred one day whilst I was out horse riding. Horse riding was one thing I had mastered ever since watching The Barefoot Indian give a breathtaking display at the circus. It was a hobby that gave me great satisfaction and I engaged in it whenever possible.

I had hired a horse on this particular day, it was a Palomino Quarter Horse and was very highly trained, I only had to think about an action and the horse responded. I rode for some time in the countryside before finding a secluded field where I could practice some manoeuvres.

I entered the field and began my session. It was going really well and the horse's ability to spin with such agility and speed made the experience even more enjoyable. The moments were flying by, it was an incredible day, the weather was perfect, as it always seemed to be these days, and the air was filled with a calmness.

The horse's talent was exhilarating and the sense soon came over me that on this day, only myself and the horse existed, every-thing else just faded into the background. This feeling was soon to be shattered! Out of the corner of my eye I spotted a young man standing at the fence and he was clapping. It would have been rude of me not to acknowledge his presence so I made my way over to him. As I approached him he said, "That was amazing! I have never seen anyone ride like that before."

"Thank you," I said in response.

"Where did you learn to ride like that?" he enquired.

"I didn't learn," I replied, "I just do what comes naturally."

He paused for a moment and then said, "Well, having seen

what I have just seen, I would like to know how to do what just comes naturally!"

"It's very easy," I said. "You just need to experience what is naturally there."

"OK," he said nonchalantly, "but how do you experience what is naturally there?"

"By experiencing it!" I replied.

A familiar puzzled look came across his face, it was a look that I had seen so many times before and I was now becoming accustomed to it.

I find the best way to get a point across is to demonstrate it so that the person can see it for themselves. For this particular demonstration I needed a flower. As I looked around it became apparent that there weren't any flowers, we were in the middle of the countryside, surrounded by fields and trees, but it was definitely lacking in the horticultural department. So me being what I am, I secretly manifested one whilst he wasn't looking.

"Look over there at that flower," I said pointing him in the direction of it.

"Where did that come from?" he asked surprised. "That wasn't there before."

"Perhaps you never noticed it before."

He didn't seem convinced at my answer, but as he couldn't come up with a logical explanation for why the flower was suddenly there, he sort of accepted my explanation.

"Go pick it and bring it back here," I said. "I want to show you something."

He made his way over to the single flower and as he did I dismounted from my horse.

"It's a daffodil," he said as he made his way back. "It's the middle of summer, daffodils don't grow in the middle of summer!"

"Well that one does," I said trying to deflect the conversation. I really should have given more thought to the manifestation, I thought to myself, however, the unexplained is not always a bad thing as it takes you beyond logic.

"Right," I said before he could say anything else. "Hold the flower and describe it to me."

"It's yellow," he said in an obvious tone.

"What else?" I enquired. "Describe it to me in detail. Don't be embarrassed, if you see it, say it."

"OK. It's yellow, it's delicate, it's stem is quite tall, there is no aroma, well, maybe just a slight one, if I look closely it has little veins running through it, it has petals that make up the whole," he paused before adding, "I can't think of anything else."

"That's OK." I said. "Now, let's look at how the flower feels, what feelings would you say it feels, what feelings does it evoke within you."

He thought about this for sometime before speaking. "Not many... I would have to say the main feeling is peace and tranquillity."

"Great!" I said in response and then continued, "You have been holding that flower for a while now and you have described it to me in detail, you've even told me what you perceive it feels."

He looked at me intently as I continued, "In all of that time did you experience the flower?"

"I am not sure I understand what you mean," he replied.

"Let me put it like this. Did you experience the flower or did you experience your thoughts about the flower?"

He thought about this and took his time over it. Finally he said, "I experienced my thoughts about it."

"That's right, you experienced your thoughts about it, your perception of it," I said. "And it is your perception of it that stops you experiencing it."

He looked at the flower again as I expanded the point. "The only thing that stops you from experiencing the flower, is your view of it. If you have a view then it is your view that you will experience!"

"But I have a view on everything!"

"Yes, you probably do and you label everything. You shroud the world with an imaginary veil of perceptions, you separate yourself from everything. Because of this it stops you experiencing that which is naturally there, in all things, yourself included. I can tell you that if you didn't hold any views, what you would experience is beyond anything that you could perceive. You would experience life as a living thing, life as it truly is. Let this be your mantra; stop perceiving, start experiencing!"

"Wow," he said and then continued, "but I am not sure what to do about my views."

"You have taken your first step which is to see that you are currently not experiencing anything, just merely engaging in your own views and perceptions. In addition, for the first time, you are entertaining the fact that there is something there to experience."

He was silent and thoughtful, but I continued, "If you are willing, try this little meditative exercise sometime, it will help you to experience exactly what I am saying."

"OK," he said excitedly, waiting for me to go on.

"Find a clock that ticks quite loudly, concentrate on the ticking sound and then after a while focus all of your attention on the space in between the tick and the tock. Or you can listen to some music and focus all of your attention on the space in between each musical note, or be aware of your breathing and focus all of your attention on the space in between the inward and outward breath. Any of these will do, the choice is yours, for with each one you will find that within that space is an experience that you have no view of and you couldn't possibly predict the experience that is there. And when you touch that space, it will blow your mind away! It is there that you will find that which comes naturally."

"I'll give that a go," he said rather excitedly. "But could I just ask you, do you experience the flower?"

"Yes, I do." I replied.

"And what does it feel like?" he asked.

"Would you like the short answer or the long answer?" I asked in reply.

"The short answer." he said quickly.

"OK. Here's the short answer," I said, "It feels complete."

"Is that it!" he said disappointed. "That doesn't really tell me anything."

"Are you sure about that?" I asked smiling.

He thought for a while then asked "Can I have the long answer?"

"Sure, but I don't think there would be enough time throughout eternity for me to get to the end of my explanation," I said laughing.

"That's OK." he said smiling. "I'll tell you to stop when I've heard enough."

"Very well," I said, "Here goes...

"When I experience a flower, it has no boundaries. It is. Isness is all it knows. The Life Force runs through its veins, there is no part in the flower where it is not. The flower *is* the Life Force. It is as though the flower is an illumination of an incredible, electrifying, vibrant, pure white light. It is light. It was never born nor shall it ever die, it simply took form. When the flower looks at you it knows all of your secrets, but could never contemplate sharing them, for to it, they are like dreams. Instead the flower smiles upon you and blesses you. It wills you to share in its biggest secret and the secret the flower holds is that it will dance in the wind for all of eternity. The flower reaches out to you. Its fragrance, beauty and innocence touches you. It touches every fiber of your being, it flows through you, to you and all around you. It shares its abundant joy. It then speaks to you, not with words, but with love, a love that is all encompassing and within that love you hear a whisper, *'you and I are one and the same'*. You suddenly feel its heart beating and you realize that it is your own heartbeat. You suddenly feel its breath expanding and you realize it is your own breath. In a single moment your spirit touches upon the soul of the flower, it is then that you realize it was the flower that touched you. Never again will you say, 'the flower is within my heart', you can only say 'I am within the heart of the flower.' Never again will you be separated. Never again will you look upon something with awe without experiencing your own innate beauty. From that moment all flows from you, all flows to you… "

"You can stop now," he suddenly interrupted.

"Oh, I was just warming up," I said smiling. "However, me sharing my experience of the flower will not lead you to your experience of it. Only you can take yourself to it!"

He looked at me, not with a puzzled look this time, but with a smile that shone from deep within.

Suddenly, it was time for him to leave, he had to get back to work, he was a farmer and had been out checking some crops when he happened to come across the field I was riding in. I said he could keep the daffodil, which pleased him. I assured him that we would meet again and with that he was off. As he walked away I could see him holding his watch up to his ear, I smiled as I knew he was probably listening to the sound of the tick tock. Only time will tell if he followed what I had suggested. (No pun intended!)

I jumped back on my horse, it was also time for me to make a move. As soon as I had mounted the horse, my ride became alert, he was ready for action. Within a split second we were off, the speed of a Quarter Horse is quite breathtaking and as always, there was no horse and rider, only the experience of an awesome energy and a singular movement remained.

I arrived back at the stables and handed my wonderful companion for the day back to its owners. I changed out of my riding gear and back into my jeans, and as I was fastening the zip I could feel the vibration of my cell phone in the back pocket. I pulled it out and read the following message:

Message from Head Office:

If you can understand the miracle of a flower, your life would change forever.

Also, we would just like to say, for no particular reason, all things which are made of parts eventually come apart.

Thinking of U xxx

I couldn't quite see the relevance of the second part of the message, however, Head Office always had the habit of saying something which would come to pass at a later date, so I just accepted that one day it would become clear as to why they were saying that.

Before leaving the stables, I rummaged through my handbag to find a treat for the horse, in doing so I noticed my notebook and it prompted me to write my notes whilst the events of the day were still fresh in my mind.

What I demonstrated today...

Find the child within

All things are equal

Life cannot be contained

Problems are whatever size you want them to be

All life is supported

All is known

Obstacles turn your life around

Eyes do not need to see in order to see

Love is all around

Many are knocking at the door, but few enter

Cell phones are not for the simple minded!

The world is like a classroom

There is only 'one'

Miracles are everywhere

All life is free to be

The only permission to seek is that of your own

I can make soup!

Give and you will receive

To experience peace - stop disturbing it!

The smallest thing can reveal the greatest thing

The unalterable is unalterable

I have amazing friends

There is only light

Impressions do not impress

All thoughts are temporary

All emotions will be erased

Life resides beyond perceptions

A flower is life manifested

Chapter 11

EVERYTHING CHANGES BUT YOU!

My longing to return to Head Office was becoming stronger and stronger as the months and years passed by, yet there was still no indication of when I would be returning. Since beginning Level 2, which now seemed like a lifetime, I was confident that I was making good progress.

Along the way I had met with some very colorful people and engaged in some extraordinary situations, all of which enabled me to demonstrate the reality of the 'Unlimited' and in doing so, awakened and stirred the hearts of those around me.

I was finding it hard to understand why I had not yet passed the task, the thought had crossed my mind that perhaps I was destined to never return, but that was too absurd to even contemplate so I dropped that thought immediately.

Throughout my adventure, apart from my time at the mansion, I had been constantly traveling around. It was great fun and no two days were the same, though suddenly I had arrived at a point where I felt I needed a permanent residence. I needed a base. I didn't regret giving up my original home as it was right to do so at the time, but now I needed to get another home. That was my next project; to find a new house, so I started to contemplate it.

As it is in the nature of thought to take form, I didn't have to wait long before my new home manifested itself to me. The brickwork was painted white and the house was set within a mature garden which surrounded the property. It was a spacious house, but not too big and it was on one level with Georgian style windows which allowed the light to flood into every room. It was perfect in every way, however, what made it extra special was the location. It was situated on a beautiful island and from the windows I could see the sea and would watch as the landscape changed and moved in a never ending cycle. The island was a place that I had visited many times before and I adored it, the scenery was stunning, the countryside was peaceful and no matter where you were on the island you were only ever a stone's throw away from the beach. It was ideal and I felt at home, but all the while I knew it was only my second home, it was a temporary measure until I could go back to Head Office, my true home.

I moved in and began to make it my own. It took me a few months to get it just how I wanted it and my time was spent being preoccupied with decorators, color swatches, fabrics and sofas.

Although I was busy with settling in, not a day went by when I wasn't given the opportunity to continue to demonstrate all that I am. Each day brought with it circumstances where I had to shine, like the time when one of the carpenters cut his finger with a Stanley knife, and to his astonishment, the wound healed up the moment I touched it. Then there was another occasion when the decorator suggested painting a wooden door to cover the garish blue that the previous occupants had painted it. He wanted to paint it white so I agreed that he could do this and he set about painting it. The next morning when he arrived the garish blue began to show through the white, so, again, he proceeded to put on another coat of white paint. The next day the same thing happened, the blue was showing through and rather irritated by this he put on another coat of white paint. This continued over a period of about five days and I quietly observed him becoming more and more frustrated. Finally, when his patience had run out, I sat him down to have a chat. "Why are you so irritated?" I asked him.

"It's that door. No matter how many coats of white paint I put on it, that horrible blue color starts to shine through it," he declared.

"So you don't like the blue then?" I asked.

"Of course not, it's awful, it's vile. Don't you agree?"

I didn't answer him, but continued with the conversation. "How many times in your life have you not liked something and have tried to whitewash over it?"

He didn't reply, but looked at me questioningly so I continued. "How many times have you encountered things you do not like and would wish to change them? How many times have you encountered situations you would wish to be free from?" I asked.

"Lots of times." he replied with a tone of despair.

"And what did you do?"

"I set about changing things," he said.

"And were you successful?"

"Yes, I think so," he replied, but with some uncertainty in his voice.

"And are you happy with the changes that you made?" I asked.

He took his time in answering me and after giving it some thought he replied, "No. I am not happy with the changes."

"Why is that?" I enquired.

Again, he gave some serious thought to his answer and then finally said, "It is hard to say why, but it seems that whenever I have made a change I always end up in the same situation. It is like history repeats itself, over and over again. Time after time I find myself in the same dilemma." He fell silent, looked at me and waited for me to say something; so I did.

"Change is an illusion, you are deceiving yourself if you think you can change anything."

He looked at me with a blank expression.

"It is like this," I continued, "I have been observing you and you have tried many times to paint that door. You have tried unsuccessfully to change it from blue to white. Each time you try to whitewash it the blue shines through, it reminds you of what you are trying to get rid of."

"That's true!" he interrupted.

"Now, there may come a time when you are successful and finally the blue stops shining through and the door is gleaming in white paint. It looks perfect."

"That's what I am aiming for!" he said laughing.

"That maybe so," I said. "But what you have to remember is that you can never really succeed in getting rid of the blue paint."

"I can't?"

"No," I replied. "No matter how many coats of paint you slap on to cover up what's there, the blue paint will always be underneath and every time you admire the whitewash, it will remind you of what lies beneath.

"And so it is with your life. Each time you try to change something, your attention will always be on the very thing that you are trying to get rid of. You are merely trying to push something away, pushing it deeper and eventually, because that's the way it is, at some point it will rise to the surface."

The man absorbed this and then said in a surprised voice. "I can see that! That is exactly what I have been doing in my life. But what do I do about it?"

"Let's take the door as an example," I said. "If you really want change then you have to go about change in the true way."

"What's the true way?" he asked suddenly excited.

"The true change takes place by stripping back all the layers of paint, by doing this it will take you back to the original, the source. What you will find there will amaze you and then and only then can you can decide if it needs painting, if it needs to change."

The man fell into deep thought. He was contemplating our conversation. Finally he spoke.

"So to summarize," he said, "if there is something I don't like and would like to change it, rather than try to whitewash over it and add layers to it, I need to look deeper and see what is underneath."

"You've got it!" I said in response.

"Great," he said. "I shall try that."

"Well, what better way to start than by using the door as a

tool," I said. "By doing this you can observe the principle and then you can apply it in your life."

He remained seated whilst he thought about the door.

"What are you waiting for?" I said, "Start stripping – the door, that is!"

He immediately stood up and began work on the door. I left him to it and went out for the rest of the afternoon.

When I returned the decorator was stood in the kitchen and his face was beaming.

"Come and have a look at the door," he said excitedly, leading the way.

I followed him to the door.

"You were right," he said. "I was amazed at what was there when I stripped away the layers of paint!"

The door, removed of all the paint, stood in its original state. It was antique solid oak and stood proud as though relieved to be finally revealed. Each knot and grain created its own unique mark, it had a timeless quality, at last it was allowed to breath and its true state was exposed.

"Isn't it beautiful?" asked the decorator.

"It is," I replied smiling. "Now that you have seen the original, that which was there all the time, is there anything you would like to change about it?"

"Absolutely not!" he declared. "It is perfect, it is beautiful in everyway. How could anybody try to hide something so magnificent?"

"They could but try!" I said. "But no matter how many changes the door appeared to go through, its true self was always there; unchanged, unaltered and perfect in all its glory."

I paused for a moment and then continued, "And so it is with you, you can try to change the changeless, but you are forever what you are. Revert to your natural state."

"I will," he said with determination.

That evening I sat and admired the door. It was stripped bare, its natural beauty was evident for all to see, it was omnipresent in the room, its fragrance permeated all around and I breathed in its aroma. At last its beauty and reverence was on show, it was no longer hidden by layers of ignorance.

That was a job well done, I thought to myself proudly, in more ways than one.

Eventually after hours of marvelling at the solid oak door, I reached for my notebook and pen and wrote:

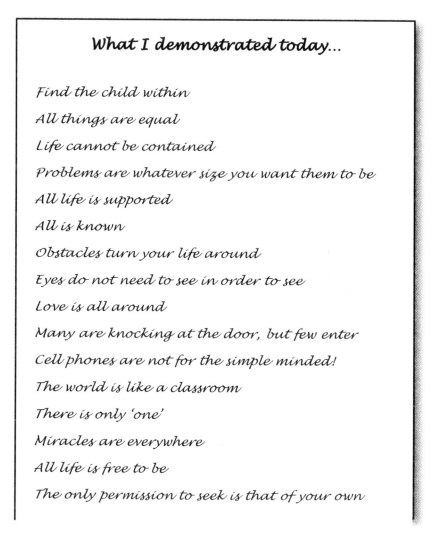

What I demonstrated today...

Find the child within

All things are equal

Life cannot be contained

Problems are whatever size you want them to be

All life is supported

All is known

Obstacles turn your life around

Eyes do not need to see in order to see

Love is all around

Many are knocking at the door, but few enter

Cell phones are not for the simple minded!

The world is like a classroom

There is only 'one'

Miracles are everywhere

All life is free to be

The only permission to seek is that of your own

I can make soup!

Give and you will receive

To experience peace - stop disturbing it!

The smallest thing can reveal the greatest thing

The unalterable is unalterable

I have amazing friends

There is only light

Impressions do not impress

All thoughts are temporary

All Emotions will be erased

Life resides beyond perceptions

A flower is life manifested

The changeless is changeless!

I had just finished writing when something peculiar happened. My cell phone began to ring, but it was now playing a new tune. It took me a few moments to recognize the tune, it was *'You Raise me up'*. How sweet, I thought as I opened the message:

Message from Head Office:

As we always say - you can't make a silk purse out of a sow's ear, and equally as important - you can't make a sow's ear out of a silk purse!
Have you received your invitation yet?
Lov alw xxx

Invitation? What's that all about? I questioned to myself. My imagination began to take off , it must be an invitation to go back to Head Office, but why would I be invited? My mind came up with all sorts of possibilities, yet in the end I gave up trying to figure it out. I would just have to be patient and wait for the intriguing invitation to arrive.

I didn't have to wait long, the following morning it was sitting on my doorstep.

Invitation from Head Office

To show our appreciation for all of the good deeds you have done, we thought it would be a nice gesture to throw a party.
We, therefore, are going to organise a BBQ for you.
We will inform you of the time and place in due course.

RSVP

A BBQ! I wasn't sure how to take that. I did think that after so many years away and all of the effort I had put into this task, that I was just a little bit more deserving than a BBQ! Maybe a banquet would have been more appropriate or the killing of the fatted calf at least, but no, all I'll be getting is a few sausages and a chicken drumstick, I thought to myself. I didn't know whether to laugh or cry! However, on reflection, I decided that one shouldn't judge and as we always say, it is the thought that counts.

When I was getting my head around the BBQ thing I prepared a text to accept the invitation. As I was doing so the thought suddenly occurred to me that perhaps the BBQ would be at Head Office, after all, they were very vague about the time and place. 'Of course!' I thought, 'it all makes sense now, I will be returning and the BBQ is their way of celebrating my return.' With excitement I sent the text off, accepting the invitation with gratitude.

Chapter 12

IT'S MY PARTY AND I'LL CRY
IF I WANT TO...

I had heard no more from Head Office regarding the BBQ, however, this was not unusual, they were so wrapped up in eternity that time means nothing to them and when they say 'in due course' this could be months, even years away. So, as usual I just pushed it to the back of my mind, progressed with my destiny and continued to demonstrate and experience all that I am. I seemed to be increasingly busy and each day brought more and more people my way with situations that were truly enlightening. It was great fun and, as usual, with each passing moment it gave me the opportunity to delve deeper and learn about myself like never before. There was never a moment when I was stuck for words or unsure as to what to do in a particular situation, for when you are in touch with the source of everything, the 'Unlimited' your words and actions just flow from you. Fear of reactions or rejections were a distant memory for me, for I knew with certainty that anything I said or did would be perfect in any given moment, all that was required of me was to breathe life into everyone and everything, and where was the fear in that?

Heaven was truly laid out before me; heaven was wherever I was because my heart was heavenly. The world was like a huge mirror, whatever was within my heart was made visible without. Life was perfect and perfection was everywhere, except for one thing – I was becoming more and more desperate to return to Head Office, I would even have to say that I was officially home sick, but as yet there was no further news from them about my return.

One morning I was sitting in the garden, it was very early as I wanted to catch the birds singing for the dawn chorus, it was such a marvellous event that I quite often sat outside to hear it. The first bird would begin to sing and then after a short time they were all joining in and the beautiful sound that they created, although deafening, in a strange way was very peaceful, it signalled a new day, a new beginning and always left me feeling ready to face the challenges of each day.

As I was marvelling at our little feathered friends and smiling to myself as they tried to compete with each other to see who could chirp the loudest, I was interrupted by my cell phone, it was letting me know that I had a text message. It was unusual to receive a message so early in the day, so I was very curious to read it. Ignoring the birds, I eagerly opened the text. It was from Head Office (of course) giving me the details of the BBQ. It was scheduled for that afternoon. 'That's typical!' I thought to myself, 'I wait all this time and then finally they give me a few hours' notice.' As I was flapping about the lack of notice, suddenly an excitement came over me, 'This is it!' I thought, 'I'm on my way home, back to where I belong.' But my excitement was soon curbed when I read where it was to be held, the location was not at Head Office, but a few miles down the road in the grounds of a large hotel.

I stared at the text for what seemed like ages, I couldn't quite get my head around what this BBQ was all about, I had no idea who would be there or why. However, I did know that I wasn't going back to Head Office and I felt deflated once again, in a resigned kind of way.

The birds were in full swing now, yet even they didn't raise my spirits, suddenly I had a lot to think about – what to wear for one! There were only six hours to go until the BBQ which didn't give me much time and I needed to start to get ready, so, I left the garden, returned indoors and hopped in the shower. I was contemplating what outfit to wear when, as I was stepping out of the shower, my thoughts were interrupted by an impatient knocking at the front door. I quickly grabbed a towel and went to answer it. There, on the doorstep, stood a very smartly dressed man.

"Hello," he said abruptly. "I want your help."

"Oh," I said in surprise and before I could say anything else he walked straight in, uninvited.

The man made himself at home in the kitchen and spoke non-stop for the next few hours, nothing interesting was said, it was all about him. I concluded from what he was saying that he was a very successful business man, clearly very wealthy and, by his tone, he was used to getting his own way. He gave no thought to the fact that I was sitting there in a towel, drip drying, all he could talk about was what he had achieved and what he hoped to achieve. Eventually, I had heard enough so I interrupted him.

"Why have you come here? What do you want from me?"

"Well," he said, "I have heard on the grapevine that you know a thing or two and with your knowledge and with my money I could really go places, I could conquer the world."

"Oh really," I said in surprise and then added, "It is obvious to me that you can't even conquer yourself, so how could you possibly conquer the world?"

The man was silent as he looked at me blankly, it was now my turn to speak.

"Let me tell you a story."

He continued to look at me blankly.

"There was a man who one day came across an apple tree and the tree was bursting with apples, each apple looked delicious and was ripe for picking. The man looked at the apples and decided there and then to pick them all before anybody else got to them. It was a long and arduous task, but eventually he had gathered them all and he felt very proud of himself. There were far too many apples for him to eat so he decided to store them and as he was doing so he couldn't help but feel that he had achieved something, not least that no one else would get the apples as he had got there first. A year passed and once again he found himself walking past the same apple tree, to his delight the tree was bursting with fruit. Again, he set about picking all of the apples before anyone else could get to them, this time it took him longer as there were more apples than the previous year and he found it more tiring, yet pride overtook the tiredness and he stored the apples along with the previous year's harvest. This went on year after year, the man, eager to get to the apple tree first, picked all the fruit and stored them in a safe place. Eventually, the man became too old and weary to pick any more apples so he decided to be happy with what he had in store and went to the barn to look at the harvest, but to his horror he found that every apple was rotten. He was distraught and in his disappointment he suddenly realized that he had never tasted one of the apples, all that effort was for nothing. He never got to taste the succulent fruit and savor the sweet, refreshing juice from them and in his zeal to keep all the apples to himself he denied anyone else from tasting them. The man then died, however, the tree continued to bear fruit year after year."

I paused and the man impatiently jumped in by asking, "So, what's the moral of this story?"

"The moral of this story is this, however grand you might think your plans are, they will never bear fruit," I replied smiling.

Again, the man was silent for a short time and then asked defiantly. "So, are you are going to share your wisdom with me or not?"

"I just did," I replied.

The man stood up as if to leave and as he did he said, "You speak in riddles!"

I turned to him and said light heartedly, "Only the clueless call clues riddles!"

The man was not amused so I quickly changed the subject. "Look," I said, "I am going to a BBQ shortly, why don't you join me, I am sure you will enjoy it, it could even be an enlightening event."

"No thank you," he said abruptly as he made his way to the door. "I have got better things to do."

"Very well," I said, "But I'd like to share this final 'riddle' with you before you go."

"OK," he said in a resigned tone.

"Your heart will always be where your riches are," I said.

He then left.

I was running so late by now that I didn't have time to think about what to wear, I just grabbed the first thing that came to hand. As I was putting on my dress, I couldn't help but think about the man that had just left my house. My thoughts were interrupted again by my cell phone ringing. In a rush I picked it up to read the message.

Message from Head Office:

Nothing is enough for the man to whom enough is too little!
C U soon
P.S. Your late! xxx

Finally, despite the morning that I had just had, I arrived at the hotel where the BBQ was being held. Again, I couldn't help wonder what it was all in aid of, 'Would anyone be there from Head Office?' I asked myself. 'I guess I will soon find out,' I thought, as I made my way across the hotel car park towards the grounds at the back where the event was to take place.

I walked through the arched gateway that led to the grounds and was completely gobsmacked at what laid before me. My jaw dropped and I felt rooted to the spot as I took in the awesome sight that I was looking at. This was no ordinary BBQ, there was not a hamburger in sight, it was a banquet fit for royalty. As I quickly glanced around I saw hog roasts, salad bars, chefs cooking the best salmon on open grills and pastry chefs busy creating works of art with spun sugar. The smell from the food was divine and it was hard for me to take it all in. The tables, dressed with white linen, were laid with the finest silver cutlery and an ornate flower arrangement sat on each one, it looked more like a lavish wedding party than a BBQ. I stood for ages in awe of what I was seeing, trying to absorb every detail, before finally making my way over to the marquee where I could hear voices and I suspected that the guests were inside waiting, after all it was where the drinks were being served. I gingerly entered as I had no idea who would be inside and I hoped my arrival would go unnoticed as I was slightly embarrassed at being late.

As I stood at the entrance to the marquee and peeped inside, I was overwhelmed. The marquee was full of familiar faces, the room was full of all the people who I had met along my journey and suddenly it made sense, why, on all those occasions I had felt compelled to say that we would meet again. As I made my way in they let out a little cheer which seemed to signal the start of the party and the orchestra began to play. (Yes, there was even an orchestra!).

I was speechless, my head was spinning with questions, 'How did all these people get here? Why are all these people here?' After a short while, I began to compose myself as people began to make their way over to me. I was thrilled to see them all and within the hour even more people had arrived and the place was heaving. I had forgotten just how many people I had met along the way. Unfortunately though, there was no one present from Head Office.

The weather was perfect for a BBQ (of course it would be!). 'Only Head Office could put on such an event,' I thought to myself. The party got into full swing, everyone was enjoying every moment, they were dancing, mingling, eating and drinking, laughter filled the air and it was wonderful to hear. As I glanced around at everyone, I was filled with pride for it was evident just how far they had all come, you could see it in their faces, their eyes were alive and the 'Unlimited' was smiling from within each of them. I was having a fantastic time, in addition to reminiscing about the wonderful times we had spent together. I delighted in hearing their stories of what adventures had happened to them after I had left them. And, of course, I was curious to know how and why they were all here. It emerged that they had all received an invitation for a 'celebration,' although none of us were any wiser as to what we were meant to be celebrating, yet that didn't matter, we celebrated anyway!

As I was socializing and moving around from person to person, suddenly, something caught my eye. I looked towards the arched gateway and saw a figure standing there, it was the wealthy man that had come to me earlier in the day. I was delighted that he had decided to come. He was glancing around, but didn't see me so I made my way over to him, yet as I did, he turned around and left. What a shame, I thought to myself, he obviously has got better things to do after all.

I found it slightly ironic, as on many occasions I had been asked, 'What is heaven like?' and I had replied 'Heaven is like a huge party that is taking place right here, right now and everyone is invited. At this party there is an abundance of food and drink, there is music, there is dancing. The room is full of fragrant, colourful, vibrant flowers. Laughter fills the air and there is joy. Everything is laid out before you. It is perfect.' Then I would be asked, 'Why can't I experience it?' And I would say 'You can! You are invited, but you have decided not to attend, you have other plans, you have got better things to do.'

As I recounted this in my mind, I couldn't help but think how near the man was to paradise, yet he was so far away. If only he would realize that the one thing he ever wanted, the one thing he truly desired was only a breath away, and a change of heart was all that was required to experience it. There was a battle going on, but only within himself. The battle commenced when running from fear to living in hope. It is a losing battle. There was nothing I could do.

Anyway, the party progressed and the wine flowed freely and in everyone's merriment it was suggested that I give a speech. I resisted this as much as I possibly could, yet they were having none of it. I really don't like giving speeches, however, as I was guest of honor I couldn't see a way out of it. I took my place on the stage, opened my mouth and allowed the words to come forth.

As the speech came to an end, which went well judging by the applause I received, there was a moment when, as I stood there looking down upon the crowd, it really struck me just how far, not only they had come, but just how far I had come in demonstrating and expressing all that I am. For the first time I could see that I had been a light, a beacon, and now all these people in front of me were shining too. It was quite a profound moment for me as the full realization started to sink in. I had done so much, I had manifested and revealed all that there is, I had put it on display for all to see. Suddenly, I knew what it was to be the Living God, to be the 'Unlimited' in action. In that moment I fully understood the true meaning of love, the true meaning of compassion, the true meaning of greatness. I was all of those things and more, I was boundless with possibilities, I was the life everlasting, the infinite and I could see all of these things in everyone standing before me.

In that moment, all became clear, for it dawned on me what we were all here to celebrate; The beautiful, the magical, the mysterious and the astonishing force which is Life itself.

I started to feel a lump in my throat and tears were beginning to well up in my eyes, everyone went blurry, so I made a quick dash to find somewhere quiet as I needed to compose myself. I found an empty table in the corner of the grounds and sat for a while to reflect. I fumbled around in my handbag to find a tissue to wipe my eyes and in doing so I pulled out my notebook, I decided to write in it.

What I demonstrated today...

Find the child within

All things are equal

Life cannot be contained

Problems are whatever size you want them to be

All life is supported

All is known

Obstacles turn your life around

Eyes do not need to see in order to see

Love is all around

Many are knocking at the door, but few enter

Cell phones are not for the simple minded!

The world is like a classroom

There is only 'one'

Miracles are everywhere

All life is free to be

The only permission to seek is that of your own

I can make soup!

Give and you will receive

To experience peace - stop disturbing it!

The smallest thing can reveal the greatest thing

The unalterable is unalterable

I have amazing friends

There is only light

Impressions do not impress

All thoughts are temporary

All Emotions will be erased

Life resides beyond perceptions

A flower is life manifested

The changeless is changeless!

You can't take from that which freely gives

Possessions are only obsessions

Perfection is a breath away - sigh into it

Earth is in heaven

The only battle is with yourself

Life is everything and everything is life

The journey from here to eternity is mo...

As I was writing I was interrupted by a woman who approached me so I stopped writing in mid-flow and quickly slipped the notebook back into my handbag. It took me a few moments to recognize her, she was one of the children who were playing in the park on the very first day that I had left Head Office. She was all grown up now with children of her own.

"Hi," she said as she sat down next to me. "Are you OK?"

"I am fine," I replied. "I just needed a moment to reflect."

"And have you reflected?" she asked.

"Yes, I have," I said smiling. "I have come to a wise conclusion."

"And what is that?" she enquired.

"I have concluded that my work here is done. There is no more that I can do here, I have achieved what I set out to achieve and I have completed my task successfully!"

"So what will you do now?" she asked.

"I am not sure." I replied. "I guess I will have to wait to hear from Head Office, wait for them to tell me that I can return. Maybe they don't think I am ready yet."

She looked thoughtful and then asked, "Can I say something?"

"Of course!"

"As you are the 'Unlimited,' that which is free from limitations, why are you waiting for Head Office to tell you when you can return? Surely it is down to you when you return!" she declared.

Her words hit me like dynamite, it was as though she had slapped me in the face. 'She's right!' I thought to myself, 'how stupid of me,' (I told you I was still dim). 'It is down to me!' There are no rules or regulations. There is no one other than I that could determine my fate. How could I have been so blind? I had been waiting what seemed like a lifetime to return, when all along the decision to return was mine, only when I concluded I was ready to go home would I be going home. For the first time ever I was stuck for words, I could only turn to her and say, "Thank you!"

No sooner had the words left my mouth, than the strangest thing started to happen. I heard a voice calling me. I glanced around to the direction of the voice, and as I did so the sun caught my eye. It was just beginning its nightly ritual of setting, the light was beginning to fade, but as I looked towards the sky I saw a shaft of brilliant white light beaming down as though someone was shining a torch. Although it seemed to be coming from the sky, it wasn't, it was not possible to describe where it was coming from, I couldn't place it. As I focused my eyes on the beam of light which was now becoming wider and brighter, I began to see a figure emerging from it and it was moving towards me. After a few moments I could clearly see who it was. It was JC. My heart leapt.

I briefly turned away from the light to look at the woman sitting next to me and it was evident that she had not, or could not see JC or the light. I quickly glanced around at all the other guests and I could tell that they could not see them either. My attention was drawn back to JC and the dazzling light. I felt compelled to walk towards him. As I did, I began to hear music and the sound of a solo singer beginning to sing *Time to Say Goodbye.*, I was not quite sure where it was coming from – the orchestra, the light or indeed my cell phone, but I was too preoccupied to care, all I remember was that it made me smile, as for some strange reason, it seemed very appropriate.

"What took you so long?" JC said laughing as I was nearing him.

I was speechless, not by his words, but by the whole incredible experience that was unfolding before me.

Realizing I was speechless, he added, "I said we would come for you when your task was completed!"

"It is time to say goodbye. We have come to take you home."

On hearing him, I couldn't help but think back to when he had said that to me on the day I was leaving Head Office and how I had totally misunderstood his words, I had assumed that they would let me know when the task was completed, not that I would decide when my task was done.

As I was thinking this, other figures began to emerge from within the dazzling tunnel of light, amongst many others The Barefoot Indian was there, she too had come to welcome me home. What radiated from them was indescribable, it was new to me, I had never experienced it before and it alighted every cell of my body. It was love, but a love that penetrated so deep within me, it touched a part of me that I had never known existed. My heart felt as though it was exploding with happiness and tears started to pour down my face, they were uncontrollable, I was crying with joy. I moved further towards the light and as I did so my body began to vibrate as though I was being absorbed into it. I looked down at my body and it was becoming lighter and brighter. I could only presume that the guests at the party were seeing me become invisible before their very eyes, but to me my body was becoming more defined, solid and alive with light, it felt real, more real than it had ever felt. It was changing, it was altering to another state of being and I was moving to another level. I knew with certainty that soon it would be done, I would be home.

I turned to all the guests who had now gathered on the lawn, all eyes were on me and their jaws were dropping, they still couldn't see the shaft of light or my wonderful friends that had come to greet me. All they could see was me ascending and disappearing before them, it was as though I was fading into the ether.

With tears streaming down my face I could hardly speak, yet I just had to say goodbye. "I am going now, but before I depart," I said through my sobbing, "I want to leave you with a final thought, one which I think is really important."

The music continued and the singer kept singing. "Only concern yourself with what comes from you," I said. "For if you were to stand on the highest mountain and shout 'I am God', the echo which comes back to you from everywhere is, 'I am God'. And if you were to stand on the highest mountain and shout 'I love you', the echo which comes back to you from everywhere is, 'I love you'. So you see, whatever comes from you is what comes to you. Understand this principle and you understand everything."

They said nothing, though they nodded slightly in acknowledgement, their eyes were still transfixed on me.

"Goodbye," I said through my tears. "I thank you all."

With that, I turned again to the shaft of light and began to walk further towards my friends, knowing that I was moments away from being reunited with them, forever.

As I was nearing them I suddenly realized that I had left my handbag on the chair. 'Damn!' I thought to myself, 'I've not finished writing in my notebook, the last entry is incomplete!' And for a split second I thought about returning to collect it. 'Don't be stupid,' I thought, 'it's too late to go back now, this is hardly the right time to be concerned with a notebook!'

Perhaps, on reflection, it wasn't the handbag or the notebook that I really wanted to go back for, I think it was more to do with my desire to keep shining, to continue to demonstrate the 'Unlimited' reality of life, but I knew with all my heart that it was time for all those wonderful people that I was leaving behind to continue with their destiny. It was their time to be a 'light unto the world', for my time was done. My heart was now destined to radiate in another place and time, on another level, in another corner of paradise.

I soon dropped the idea of returning for my handbag and raced towards my friends who, with open arms, were waiting patiently and serenely in the brilliant light. As I finally approached them I gave one final glance backwards and I knew that the amazing people I had met along my incredible journey could no longer see me. I was home...

So there you have it, I was home once more, back in the place which had never left me and I was looking forward to my next chapter in the ongoingness of life. But just one final thing before we meet again, if you do happen to stumble across my brown leather designer handbag, treat it as your own. You will know it's my bag because it is crammed full of things, amongst which are some boiled sweets (don't eat them, they are way past their sell by date!), a cell phone with a mind of its own, and a notebook. Please feel free to add to the notebook, feel free to finish the last entry, but whatever you do with it, cherish it, learn from it, pass it on and share it, for it will lead you to where you really want to be; the place where every tear is wiped away and you will cry no more.

Until then...

x

For further information about the author and her other books please visit

www.juliaheywood.co.uk

BOOKS

O is a symbol of the world, of oneness and unity. In different cultures it also means the "eye," symbolizing knowledge and insight. We aim to publish books that are accessible, constructive and that challenge accepted opinion, both that of academia and the "moral majority."

Our books are available in all good English language bookstores worldwide. If you don't see the book on the shelves ask the bookstore to order it for you, quoting the ISBN number and title. Alternatively you can order online (all major online retail sites carry our titles) or contact the distributor in the relevant country, listed on the copyright page.

See our website www.o-books.net for a full list of over 500 titles, growing by 100 a year.

And tune in to myspiritradio.com for our book review radio show, hosted by June-Elleni Laine, where you can listen to the authors discussing their books.

MySpiritRadio